PLUM PIE

'Who is Valerie Fanshawe?' asked Lord
Emsworth.

'The daughter of Colonel Fanshawe of
Marling Hall, the tally-ho and view-halloo chap.
Haven't you met him?' said Gally.

'No,' said Lord Emsworth, who never met
anyone, if he could help it. 'But why should
Frances object to Frederick giving this young
woman a dog?'

'I didn't say *a* dog, I said *her* dog, whom she
loves to distraction. However, that could be
straightened out, I imagine, with a few kisses
and a remorseful word or two if Valerie
Fanshawe were a girl with a pasty face and
spectacles, but unfortunately she isn't. She
looks like something out of a beauty chorus.
Let Aggie get one glimpse of Valerie Fanshawe
and learn that Freddie has been showering
dogs on her, and she'll probably divorce him.'

'Bless my soul. What would Frederick do
then?'

'I suppose he would come and live here.'

'What, at the castle?' cried Lord Emsworth,
appalled. 'Good God!'

Plum Pie

P. G. Wodehouse

CORONET BOOKS
Hodder and Stoughton

Copyright © P. G. Wodehouse 1966

First published 1966 by Herbert Jenkins Limited

'Success Story' © 1950 P. G. Wodehouse
first published in *Nothing Serious*

Coronet edition, revised and amended, 1978
Second impression 1983

Printed and bound in Great Britain for
Hodder and Stoughton Paperbacks, a
division of Hodder and Stoughton Ltd.,
Mill Road, Dunton Green, Sevenoaks,
Kent (Editorial Office: 47 Bedford
Square, London, WC1 3DP) by
Cox & Wyman Ltd., Reading

ISBN 0 340 22694 3

CONTENTS

* 1 *

Jeeves and the Greasy Bird

The shades of night were falling fairly fast as I latchkeyed self and suitcase into the Wooster G.H.Q. Jeeves was in the sitting room messing about with holly, for we would soon be having Christmas at our throats and he is always a stickler for doing the right thing. I gave him a cheery greeting.

'Well, Jeeves, here I am, back again.'

'Good evening, sir. Did you have a pleasant visit?'

'Not too bad. But I'm glad to be home. What was it the fellow said about home?'

'If your allusion is to the American poet John Howard Payne, sir, he compared it to its advantage with pleasures and palaces. He called it sweet and said there was no place like it.'

'And he wasn't so far out. Shrewd chap, John Howard Payne.'

'I believe he gave uniform satisfaction, sir.'

I had just returned from a weekend at the Chuffnell Regis clinic of Sir Roderick Glossop, the eminent loony doctor or nerve specialist as he prefers to call himself — not, I may add, as a patient but as a guest. My Aunt Dahlia's cousin Percy had recently put in there for repairs, and she had asked me to pop down and see how he was making out. He had got the idea, I don't know why, that he was being followed about by little men with black beards, a state of affairs which he naturally wished to have adjusted with all possible speed.

'You know, Jeeves,' I said some moments later, as I sat quaffing the whisky-and-s with which he had supplied me, 'life's odd, you can't say it isn't. You never know where you are with it.'

'There was some particular aspect of it that you had in mind, sir?'

'I was thinking of me and Sir R. Glossop. Who would ever have thought the day would come when he and I would be hobnobbing like a couple of sailors on shore leave? There was a time, you probably remember, when he filled me with a nameless fear and I leaped like a startled grasshopper at the sound of his name. You have not forgotten?'

'No, sir, I recall that you viewed Sir Roderick with concern.'

'And he me with ditto.'

'Yes, sir, a stiffness certainly existed. There was no fusion between your souls.'

'Yet now our relations are as cordial as they can stick. The barriers that separated us have come down with a bump. I beam at him. He beams at me. He calls me Bertie. I call him Roddy. To put the thing in a nutshell, the dove of peace is in a rising market and may quite possibly go to par. Of course, like Shadrach, Meshach, and Abednego, if I've got the names right, we passed through the furnace together, and that always forms a bond.'

I was alluding to the time when — from motives I need not go into beyond saying that they were fundamentally sound — we had both blacked our faces, he with burned cork, I with boot polish, and had spent a night of terror wandering through Chuffnell Regis with no place to lay our heads, as the expression is. You don't remain on distant terms with somebody you've shared an experience like that with.

'But I'll tell you something about Roddy Glossop, Jeeves,' I said, having swallowed a rather grave swallow of the strengthening fluid. 'He has something on his mind. Physically I found him in excellent shape — few fiddles could have been fitter — but he was gloomy . . . distrait . . . brooding. Conversing with him, one felt that his thoughts were far away and that those thoughts were stinkers. I could hardly get a word out of him. It made me feel like that fellow in the Bible who tried to charm the deaf adder and didn't get to first base. There was a blighter named Blair Eggleston there, and it may have been this that depressed him, for this Eggleston . . . Ever hear of him? He writes books.'

'Yes, sir. Mr. Eggleston is one of our angry young novelists. The critics describe his work as frank, forthright and fearless.'

'Oh, do they? Well, whatever his literary merits he struck me as a fairly noxious specimen. What's he angry about?'

'Life, sir.'

'He disapproves of it?'

'So one would gather from his output, sir.'

'Well, I disapproved of him, which makes us all square. But I don't think it was having him around that caused the Glossop gloom. I am convinced that the thing goes deeper than that. I believe it's something to do with his love life.'

I must mention that while at Chuffnell Regis Pop Glossop, who was a widower with one daughter, had become betrothed to Myrtle, Lady Chuffnell, the aunt of my old crony Marmaduke ('Chuffy') Chuffnell, and that I should have found him still single more than a year later seemed strange to me. One would certainly have expected him by this time to have raised the price of a marriage licence and had the Bishop and assistant clergy getting their noses down to it. A redblooded loony doctor under the influence of the divine passion ought surely to have put the thing through months ago.

'Do you think they've had a row, Jeeves?'

'Sir?'

'Sir Roderick and Lady Chuffnell.'

'Oh no, sir. I am sure there is no diminution of affection on either side.'

'Then why the snag?'

'Her ladyship refuses to take part in the wedding ceremony while Sir Roderick's daughter remains unmarried, sir. She has stated in set terms that nothing will induce her to share a home with Miss Glossop. This would naturally render Sir Roderick moody and despondent.'

A bright light flashed upon me. I saw all. As usual, Jeeves had got to the very heart of the matter.

A thing that always bothers me when compiling these memoirs of mine is the problem of what steps to take when I bring on the stage a dramatis persona, as I believe the expression is, who has already appeared in some earlier instalment. Will the customers, I ask myself, remember him or her, or will they have completely forgotten her or him, in which case they will naturally want a few footnotes to put them abreast. This difficulty arises in regard to Honoria Glossop, who got into the act in what I suppose would be about Chapter Two of the Wooster Story. Some will recall her, but there may be those who will protest that they never heard of the beazel in their lives, so perhaps better be on the safe side and risk the displeasure of the blokes with good memories.

Here, then, is what I recorded with ref to this H. Glossop at the time when owing to circumstances over which I had no control we had become engaged.

'Honoria Glossop,' I wrote, 'was one of those large, strenuous dynamic girls with the physique of a middleweight catch-as-catch-can wrestler and a laugh resembling the sound made by the Scotch Express going under a bridge. The effect she had on me was to make me slide into a cellar and lie low there till they blew the All Clear.'

One could readily, therefore, understand the reluctance of Myrtle, Lady Chuffnell to team up with Sir Roderick while the above was still a member of the home circle. The stand she had taken reflected great credit on her sturdy commonsense, I considered.

A thought struck me, the thought I so often have when Jeeves starts dishing the dirt.

'How do you know all this, Jeeves? Did he confer with you?' I said, for I knew how wide his consulting practice was. 'Put it up to Jeeves' is so much the slogan in my circle of acquaintance that it might be that even Sir Roderick Glossop, finding himself on a sticky wicket, had decided to place his affairs in his hands. Jeeves is like Sherlock Holmes. The highest in the land come to him with their problems. For all I know, they may give him jewelled snuff boxes.

It appeared that I had guessed wrong.

'No, sir, I have not been honoured with Sir Roderick's confidence.'

'Then how did you find out about his spot of trouble? By extra-whatever-it's-called?'

'Extra-sensory perception? No, sir. I happened to be glancing yesterday at the G section of the club book.'

I got the gist. Jeeves belongs to a butlers and valets club in Curzon Street called the Junior Ganymede, and they have a book there in which members are required to enter information about their employers. I remember how stunned I was when he told me one day that there are eleven pages about me in it.

'The data concerning Sir Roderick and the unfortunate situation in which he finds himself were supplied by Mr. Dobson.'

'Who?'

'Sir Roderick's butler, sir.'

'Of course, yes.' I said, recalling the dignified figure into whose palm I had pressed a couple of quid on leaving that morning. 'But surely Sir Roderick didn't confide in him?'

'No, sir, but Dobson's hearing is very acute and it enabled him to learn the substance of conversations between Sir Roderick and her ladyship.'

'He listened at the keyhole?'

'So one would be disposed to imagine, sir.'

I mused awhile. So that was how the cookie crumbled. A pang of p for the toad beneath the harrow whose affairs we were discussing passed through me. It would have been plain to a far duller auditor than Bertram Wooster that poor old Roddy was in a spot. I knew how deep was his affection and esteem for Chuffy's Aunt Myrtle. Even when he was liberally coated with burned cork that night at Chuffnell Regis I had been able to detect the lovelight in his eyes as he spoke of her. And when I reflected how improbable it was that anyone would ever be ass enough to marry his daughter Honoria, thus making his path straight and ironing out the bugs in the scenario, my heart bled for him.

I mentioned this to Jeeves.

'Jeeves,' I said, 'my heart bleeds for Sir R. Glossop.'

'Yes, sir.'

'Does your heart bleed for him?'

'Profusely, sir.'

'And nothing to be done about it. We are helpless to assist.'

'One fears so, sir.'

'Life can be very sad, Jeeves.'

'Extremely, sir.'

'I'm not surprised that Blair Eggleston has taken a dislike to it.'

'No, sir.'

'Perhaps you had better bring me another whisky-and-s, to cheer me up. And after that I'll pop off to the Drones for a bite to eat.'

He gave me an apologetic look. He does this by allowing one eyebrow to flicker for a moment.

'I am sorry to say I have been remiss, sir, I inadvertently

forgot to mention that Mrs. Travers is expecting you to entertain her to dinner here tonight.'

'But isn't she at Brinkley?'

'No, sir, she has temporarily left Brinkley Court and taken up residence at her town house in order to complete her Christmas shopping.'

'And she wants me to give her dinner?'

'That was the substance of her words to me on the telephone this morning, sir.'

My gloom lightened perceptibly. This Mrs. Travers is my good and deserving Aunt Dahlia, with whom it is always a privilege and pleasure to chew the fat. I would be seeing her, of course, when I went to Brinkley for Christmas, but getting this preview was an added attraction. If anyone could take my mind off the sad case of Roddy Glossop, it was she. I looked forward to the reunion with bright anticipation. I little knew that she had a bombshell up her sleeve and would be touching it off under my trouser seat while the night was yet young.

On these occasions when she comes to town and I give her dinner at the flat there is always a good deal of gossip from Brinkley Court and neighbourhood to be got through before other subjects are broached, and she tends not to allow a nephew to get a word in edgeways. It wasn't till Jeeves had brought the coffee that any mention of Sir Roderick Glossop was made. Having lit a cigarette and sipped her first sip, she asked me how he was, and I gave her the same reply I had given Jeeves.

'In robust health,' I said, 'but gloomy. Sombre. Moody. Despondent.'

'Just because you were there, or was there some other reason?'

'He didn't tell me,' I said guardedly. I always have to be very careful not to reveal my sources when Jeeves give me information he has gleaned from the club book. The rules about preserving secrecy concerning its contents are frightfully strict at the Junior Ganymede. I don't know what happens to you if you're caught giving away inside stuff, but I should imagine that you get hauled up in a hollow square of valets and butlers and have your buttons snipped off before being formally bunged out of the institution. And it's a very comforting thought that such precautions are taken, for I should hate to think that there was any chance of those eleven pages about me receiving wide publicity. It's bad enough to know that a book like that — pure dynamite, as you might say — is in existence. 'He didn't let me in on what was eating him. He just sat there being gloomy and despondent.'

The old relative laughed one of those booming laughs of hers which in the days when she hunted with the Quorn and Pytchley probably lifted many a sportman from the saddle. Her vocal delivery when amused always resembles one of those explosives in a London street you read about in the papers.

'Well, Percy had been with him for several weeks. And then you on top of Percy. Enough to blot the sunshine from any man's life. How is Percy, by the way?'

'Quite himself again. A thing I wouldn't care to be, but no doubt it pleases him.'

'Little men no longer following him around?'

'If they are, they've shaved. He hasn't seen a black beard for quite a while, he tells me.'

'That's good. Percy'll be all right if he rid himself of the idea that alcohol is a food. Well, we'll soon buck Glossup up when he comes to Brinkley for Christmas.'

'Will he be there?'

'He certainly will, and joy will be unconfined. We're going to have a real old-fashioned Christmas with all the trimmings.'

'Holly? Mistletoe?'

'Yards of both. And a children's party complete with Santa Claus.'

'With the vicar in the stellar role?'

'No, he's down with flu.'

'The curate?'

'Sprained his ankle.'

'Then who are you going to get?'

'Oh, I'll find someone. Was anyone else at Glossop's?'

'Only a fellow of the name of Eggleston.'

'Blair Eggleston, the writer?'

'Yes, Jeeves tells me he writes books.'

'And articles. He's doing a series for me on the Modern Girl.'

For some years, helped out by doles from old Tom Travers,

her husband. Aunt Dahlia had been running a weekly paper for women called *Milady's Boudoir*, to which I once contributed a 'piece', as we journalists call it, on What The Well-Dressed Man is Wearing. The little sheet has since been sold, but at that time it was still limping along and losing its bit of money each week, a source of considerable spiritual agony to Uncle Tom, who had to foot the bills. He has the stuff in sackfuls, but he hates to part.

'I'm sorry for that boy,' said Aunt Dahlia.

'For Blair Eggleston? Why?'

'He's in love with Honoria Glossop.'

'What!' I cried. She amazed me. I wouldn't have thought it could be done.

'And is too timid to tell her so. It's often that way with these frank, fearless young novelists. They're devils on paper, but put them up against a girl who doesn't come out of their fountain pen and their feet get as cold as a dachshund's nose. You'd think, when you read his novels, that Blair Eggleston was a menace to the sex and ought to be kept on a chain in the interests of pure womanhood, but is he? No, sir. He's just a rabbit. I don't know if he has ever actually found himself in an incense-scented boudoir alone with a girl with sensual lips and dark smouldering eyes, but if he did, I'll bet he would take a chair as far away from her as possible and ask her if she had read any good books lately. Why are you looking like a half-witted fish?'

'I was thinking of something.'

'What?'

'Oh, just something.' I said warily. Her character sketch of Blair Eggleston had given me one of those ideas I do so often get quick as a flash, but I didn't want to spill it till I'd had time to think it over and ponder on it. It never does to expose these brain waves to the public eye before you've examined them from every angle. 'How do you know all this?' I said.

'He told me in a burst of confidence the other day when we were discussing his Modern Girl Series. I suppose I must have one of those sympathetic personalities which invite confidences. You will recall that you have always told me about your various love affairs.'

'That's different.'

'In what way?'

'Use the loaf, old flesh and blood. You're my aunt. A nephew naturally bares his soul to a loved aunt.'

'I see what you mean. Yes, that makes sense. You do love me dearly, don't you?'

'Like billy-o. Always have.'

'Well, I'm certainly glad to hear you say that —'

'Well deserved tribute.'

' — because there's something I want you to do for me.'

'Consider it done.'

'I want you to play Santa Claus at my children's Christmas party.'

Should I have seen it coming? Possibly. But I hadn't, and I tottered where I sat. I was trembling like an aspen. I don't know if you've even seen an aspen — I haven't myself as far as I can remember — but I knew they were noted for trembling like the dickens. I uttered a sharp cry, and she said if I was going to sing, would I kindly do it elsewhere, as her ear drum was sensitive.

'Don't say such things even in fun,' I begged her.

'I'm not joking.'

I gazed at her incredulously.

'You seriously expect me to put on white whiskers and a padded stomach and go about saying "Ho, ho, ho" to a bunch of kids as tough as those residing near your rural seat?'

'They aren't tough.'

'Pardon me. I've seen them in action. You will recollect that I was present at the recent school treat.'

'You can't go by that. Naturally they wouldn't have the Christmas spirit at a school treat in the middle of summer. You'll find them as mild as newborn lambs on Christmas Eve.'

I laughed a sharp, barking laugh.

'*I* shan't.'

'Are you trying to tell me you won't do it?'

'I am.'

She snorted emotionally and expressed the opinion that I was a worm.

'But a prudent, levelheaded worm,' I assured her. 'A worm who knows enough not to stick its neck out.'

'You really won't do it?'

'Not for all the rice in China.'

'Not to oblige a loved aunt?'

'Not to oblige a posse of loved aunts.'

'Now listen, young Bertie, you abysmal young blot . . .'

As I closed the front door behind her some twenty minutes later, I had rather the feeling you get when parting company with a tigress of the jungle or one of those fiends with hatchet who are always going about slaying six. Normally the old relative is as genial a soul as ever downed a veal cutlet, but she's apt to get hot under the collar when thwarted, and in the course of the recent meal, as we have seen, I had been compelled to thwart her like a ton of bricks. It was with quite a few beads of persp bedewing the brow that I went back to the dining room, where Jeeves was cleaning up the debris.

'Jeeves,' I said, brushing away the b of p with my cambric handkerchief, 'you were off stage towards the end of dinner, but did you happen to drink in any of the conversation that was taking place?'

'Oh yes, sir.'

'Your hearing, like Dobson's, is acute?'

'Extremely, sir. And Mrs. Travers has a robust voice, I received the impression that she was incensed.'

'She was as sore as a gumboil. And why? Because I stoutly refused to portray Santa Claus at the Christmas orgy she is giving down at Brinkley for the children of the local yokels.'

'So I gathered from her obiter dicta, sir.'

'I suppose most of the things she called me were picked up on the hunting field in her hunting days.'

'No doubt, sir.'

'Members of the Quorn and Pytchley are not guarded in their speech.'

'Very seldom, sir, I understand.'

'Well, her efforts were . . . what's that word I've heard you use?'

'Bootless, sir?'

'Or fruitless?'

'Whichever you prefer, sir.'

'I was not to be moved. I remained firm. I am not a disobliging man, Jeeves. If somebody wanted me to play Hamlet,

I would do my best to give satisfaction. But at dressing up in white whiskers and a synthetic stomach I draw the line and draw it sharply. She huffed and puffed, as you heard, but she might have known that argument would be bootless. As the wise old saying has it, you can take a horse to the water, but you can't make it play Santa Claus.'

'Very true, sir.'

'You think I was justified in being adamant?'

'Fully justified, sir.'

'Thank you, Jeeves.'

I must say I thought it pretty decent of him to give the young master the weight of his support like this, for though I haven't mentioned it before it was only a day or two since I had been compelled to thwart him as inflexibly as I had thwarted the recent aunt. He had been trying to get me to go to Florida after Christmas, handing out a lot of talk about how pleasant it would be for my many American friends, most of whom make a bee line for Hobe Sound in the winter months, to have me with them again, but I recognised this, though specious, as merely the old oil. I knew what was the thought behind his words. He likes the fishing in Florida and yearns some day to catch a tarpon.

Well, I sympathised with his sporting aspirations and would have pushed them along if I could have managed it, but I particularly wanted to be in London for the Drones Club Darts Tournament, which takes place in February and which I confidently expected to win this year, so I said Florida was out and he said 'Very good, sir', and that was that. The point I'm making is that there was no dudgeon or umbrage or anything of that sort on his part, as there would have been if he had been a lesser man, which of course he isn't.

'And yet, Jeeves,' I said, continuing to touch on the affair of the stricken aunt, 'though my firmness and resolution enabled me to emerge victorious from the battle of wills, I can't help feeling a pang.'

'Sir?'

'Of remorse. It's always apt to gnaw you when you've crushed someone beneath the iron heel. You can't help thinking that you ought to do something to bind up the wounds and bring the sunshine back into the poor slob's life. I don't like the thought of Aunt Dahlia biting her pillow tonight and trying to choke back the rising sobs because I couldn't see my way to fulfilling her hopes and dreams. I think I should extend something in the way of an olive branch or *amende honorable*.'

'It would be a graceful act, sir.'

'So I'll blow a few bob on flowers for her. Would you mind nipping out tomorrow morning and purchasing say two dozen long-stemmed roses?'

'Certainly, sir.'

'I think they'll make her face light up, don't you?'

'Unquestionably, sir, I will attend to the matter immediately after breakfast.'

'Thank you, Jeeves.'

I was smiling one of my subtle smiles as he left the room, for in the recent exchanges I had not been altogether frank, and it tickled me to think that he thought I was merely trying to apply a soothing poultice to my conscience.

Mark you, what I had said about wanting to do the square thing by the aged relative and heal the breach and all that sort of thing was perfectly true, but there was a lot more than that behind the gesture. It was imperative that I get her off the boil, because her co-operation was essential to the success of a scheme or plan or plot which had been fizzing in the Wooster brain ever since the moment after dinner when she had asked me why I was looking like a halfwitted fish. It was a plan designed to bring about the happy ending for Sir R. Glossop, and now that I had had time to give it the once over it seemed to me that it couldn't miss.

Jeeves brought the blooms while I was in my bath, and having dried the frame and donned the upholstery and breakfasted and smoked a cigarette to put heart into me I started out with them.

I wasn't expecting a warm welcome from the old flesh and blood, which was lucky, because I didn't get one. She was at her haughtiest, and the look she gave me was the sort of look which in her Quorn and Pytchley days she would have given some fellow-sportsman whom she had observed riding over hounds.

'Oh, it's you?' she said.

Well, it was, of course, no argument about that, so I endorsed her view with a civil good morning and a smile — rather a weak smile, probably, for her aspect was formidable. She was plainly sizzling.

'I hope you thoroughly understand,' she said, 'that after your craven exhibition last night I'm not speaking to you.'

'Oh, aren't you?'

'Certainly not. I'm treating you with silent contempt. What's that you've got there?'

'Some long-stemmed roses. For you.'

She sneered visibly.

'You and your long-stemmed roses! It would take more than long-stemmed roses to change my view that you're a despicable cowardy custard and a disgrace to a proud family. Your ancestors fought in the Crusades and were often mentioned in despatches, and you cringe like a slated snail at the thought of appearing as Santa Claus before an audience of charming children who wouldn't hurt a fly. It's enough to make an aunt turn her face to the wall and give up the struggle. But perhaps,' she said, her manner softening for a moment, 'you've come to tell me you've changed your mind?'

'I fear not, aged relative.'

'Then buzz off, and on your way home try if possible to get run over by a motor bus. And may I be there to hear you go pop.'

I saw that I had better come to the *res* without delay.

'Aunt Dahlia,' I said, 'It is within your power to bring happiness and joy into a human life.'

'If it's yours, I don't want to.'

'Not mine. Roddy Glossop's. Sit in with me in a plan or scheme which I have in mind, and he'll go pirouetting about his clinic like a lamb in Springtime.'

She drew a sharp breath and eyed me keenly.

'What's the time?' she asked.

I consulted the wrist-w.

'A quarter to eleven. Why?'

'I was only thinking that it's very early for anyone, even you to get pie-eyed.'

'I'm not pie-eyed.'

'Well, you're talking as if you were. Have you got a piece of chalk?'

I tut-tutted impatiently.

'Of course I haven't. Do you think I go about with pieces of
chalk on my person? What do you want it for?'

'I would like to draw a line on the carpet and see if you can
walk along it, because it's being borne in upon me more em-
phatically every moment that you're stewed to the gills. Say
"Truly rural".'

I did so.

'And "She stood at the door of Burgess's fish sauce shop,
welcoming in." '

Again I passed the test.

'Well,' she said grudgingly, 'you seem as sober as you ever
are. What do you mean about bringing happiness and joy into
old Glossop's life?'

'The matter is susceptible of a ready explanation. I must
begin by saying that Jeeves told me a story yesterday that
shocked me to the core. No,' I said in answer to her query, 'it
was not the one about the young man of Calcutta. It had to do
with Roddy's love life. It's a long story, but I'll condense it into
short-short, and I would like to stress before embarking on my
narrative that you can rely on it being accurate, for when Jeeves
tells you anything, it's like getting it straight from the mouth of
the stable cat. Furthermore, it's substantiated by Mr. Dobson,
Roddy's butler. You know Myrtle, Lady Chuffnell?'

'I've met her.'

'She and Roddy are betrothed.'

'So I've heard.'

'They love each other fondly.'

'So what's wrong with that?'

'I'll tell you what's wrong. She stoutly declined to go centre-
aisleing with him until his daughter Honoria gets married.'

I had expected this to make her sit up, and it did. For the
first time her demeanour conveyed the impression that she
wasn't labelling my utterance as just delirious babble from the
sick bed. She has always been fond of R. Glossop and it came as
a shock to her to learn that he was so firmly established in the
soup. I wouldn't say she turned pale, for after years of following the hounds in all weathers she can't, but she snorted and
I could see that she was deeply moved.

'For heaven's sake! Is this true?'

'Jeeves has all the facts.'

'Does Jeeves know everything?'

'I believe so. Well, you can understand Ma Chuffnell's attitude. If you were a bride, would you want to have Honoria a permanent resident of your little nest?'

'I wouldn't.'

'Exactly. So obviously steps must be taken by Roddy's friends and well-wishers to get her married. And that brings me to the nub. I have a scheme.'

'I'll bet it's rotten.'

'On the contrary, it's a ball of fire. It flashed on me last night, when you were telling me that Blair Eggleston loves Honoria. That is where hope lies.'

'You mean you're thinking that he will marry her and take her off the strength?'

'Precisely.'

'Not a chance. I told you he was too much of a rabbit to suggest a merger. He'll never have the nerve to propose.'

'Unless helped by a push from behind.'

'And who's going to give him that?'

'I am. With your co-operation.'

She gave me another of those long keen looks, and I could see that she was again asking herself if her favourite nephew wasn't steeped to the tonsils in the juice of the grape. Fearing more tests and further references to pieces of chalk, I hastened to explain.

'Here's the idea. I start giving Honoria the rush of a lifetime. I lush her up at lunch and dinner. I take her to theatres and night clubs. I haunt her like a family spectre and cling to her closer than a porous plaster.'

I thought I heard her mutter 'Poor girl', but I ignored the slur and continued.

'You meanwhile ... Will you be seeing something of Eggleston?'

'I see him daily. He brings me his latest views on the Modern Girl.'

'Then the thing's in the bag. You say he has already confided in you about his warmer-and-deeper-than-ordinary-friendship feelings concerning Honoria, so it won't be difficult for you to bring the subject up in the course of conversation. You warn him in a motherly way that he's a sap if he goes on not telling his love and letting concealment like a worm in the bud feed on his damask cheek — one of Jeeves's gags. I thought he put it rather well — and stress the fact that he had better heat up his feet and grab the girl while the grabbing's good, because you happen to know that your nephew Bertram is making a heavy play in her direction and may sew up the deal at any moment. Use sufficient eloquence, and I can't see how he can fail to respond. He'll be pouring out his love before you know where you are.'

'And suppose she doesn't feel like getting engaged to him?'

'Absurd. Why, she was once engaged to *me*.'

She was silent for a space, plunged in thought, as the expression is.

'I'm not sure,' she said at length, 'that you haven't got something.'

'It's a snip.'

'Yes. I think you're right. Jeeves has a great brain.'

'What's Jeeves got to do with it?'

'Wasn't it his idea?'

I drew myself up rather haughtily — not an easy thing to do when you're sitting in an arm chair. I resent this universal tendency to take it for granted that whenever I suggest some particularly ripe scheme, it must be Jeeves's.

'The sequence was entirely mine.'

'Well, it's not at all a bad one. I've often said that you sometimes have lucid intervals.'

'And you'll sit in and do your bit?'

'It will be a pleasure.'

'Fine. Can I use your phone? I want to ask Honoria Glossop to lunch.'

I should imagine that it has often been said of Bertram Wooster that when he sets his hand to the plough he does not readily sheathe the sword. I had told Aunt Dahlia that I was going to give Honoria the rush of a lifetime, and the rush of a lifetime was precisely what I gave her. I lunched, dined and on two occasions nightclubbed her. It ran into money, but you can put up with a few punches in the pocketbook when you're working in a good cause. Even when wincing at the figures at the foot of the bill I was able to console myself with the thought of what all this was in aid of. Nor did I grudge the hours spent in the society of a girl whom in normal circs I would willingly have run a mile in tight shoes to avoid. Pop Glossop's happiness was at stake, and when a pal's happiness is at stake, the undersigned does not count the cost.

Nor were my efforts bootless. Aunt Dahlia was always ringing me up to tell me that Blair Eggleston's temperature was rising steadily day by day and it seemed to her only a question of time before the desired object would be achieved. And came a day when I was able to go to her with the gratifying news that the d.o. had indeed been a.

I found her engrossed in an Erle Stanley Gardner, but she lowered the volume courteously as I entered.

'Well, ugly,' she said, 'what brings you here? Why aren't you off somewhere with Honoria Glossop, doing your South American Joe act? What's the idea of playing hooky like this?'

I smiled one of my quiet smiles.

'Aged relative,' I said, 'I have come to inform you that I think we have reached the end of the long long trail,' and without further preamble I gave her the low-down. 'Have you been out today?'

'I went for a stroll, yes.'

'The weather probably struck you as extraordinarily mild for the latter part of December. More like spring than winter.'

'You haven't come here to talk about the weather?'

'You will find it is germane to the issue. Because the afternoon was so balmy — '

'Like others I could name.'

'I beg your pardon?'

'I didn't speak. Go on.'

'Well, as it was such a nice day I thought I would take a walk in the Park. I did so, and blowed if the first thing I saw wasn't Honoria. She was sitting on a chair by the Serpentine, I was about to duck, but it was too late. She had seen me, so I had to heave alongside and chat. And suddenly who should come along but Blair Eggleston.'

I had enchained her interest. She uttered a yip.

'He saw you?'

'With the naked eye.'

'Then that was your moment. If you'd had an ounce of sense, you'd have kissed her.'

I smiled another of my quiet ones.

'I did.'

'You *did*?'

'Yes, sir, I folded her in a close embrace and let her have it.'

'And what did Eggleston say?'

'I didn't wait to hear. I pushed off.'

'But you're sure he saw you?'

'He couldn't have missed. He was only a yard or two away, and the visibility was good.'

It isn't often that I get unstinted praise from my late father's sister, she as a rule being my best friend and severest critic, but on this occasion she gave me a rave notice. It was a pleasure to listen to her.

'That should have done it,' she said after handing me some stately compliments on my ingenuity and resource. 'I saw Eggleston yesterday, and when I mentioned what fun you and Honoria were having going about together, he looked like a blond Othello. His hands were clenched, his eyes burning, and if he wasn't grinding his teeth, I don't know a ground tooth when I hear one. That kiss was just what he needed to push him over the edge. He probably proposed to her the moment you were out of the way.'

'That's how I had it figured out.'

'Oh, hell,' said the old ancestor, for at this moment the telephone rang, interrupting us just when we wanted to go on discussing the thing undisturbed. She reached for it, and a long onesided conversation ensued. I say onesided because her contribution to it consisted merely of Ohs and Whats. Eventually whoever was at the other end appeared to have said his or her say, for she replaced ths receiver and turned a grave face in my direction.

'That was Honoria,' she said.

'Oh, really?'

'And what she had to tell me was fraught with interest.'

'Did matters work out according to plan?'

'Not altogether.'

'How do you mean, not altogether?'

'Well, to begin with, it seems that Blair Eggleston, no doubt inflamed by what I told you I had said to him yesterday, proposed to her last night.'

'He did?'

'And was accepted.'

'That's good.'

'Not so good.'

'Why not?'

'Because when he saw you kiss her, he blew his top and broke the engagement.'

'Oh, my God!'

'Nor is that all. The worst is yet to come. She now says she's going to marry you. She said she quite realised your many defects but is sure she can correct them and mould you, and even though you aren't the mate of her dreams, she feels that your patient love should be rewarded. Obviously what happened was that you made yourself too fascinating. There was always that risk, I suppose.'

Long before she had concluded these remarks I had gone into my aspen act again. I goggled at her, stunned.

'But this is frightful!'

'I told you it wasn't so good.'

'You aren't pulling my leg?'

'No, it's official.'

'Then what shall I do for the best?'

She shrugged a moody shoulder.

'Don't ask me,' she said. 'Consult Jeeves. He may be able to suggest something.'

Well, it was all very well to say consult Jeeves, but it wasn't as simple as she seemed to think. The way I looked at it was that to place him in possession of the facts in what you might call pitiless detail would come under the head of bandying a woman's name, which, as everybody knows, is the sort of thing that gets you kicked out of clubs and cut by the County. On the other hand, to be in a jam like this and not seek his counsel would be a loony proceeding. It was only after profound thought that I saw how the thing could be worked. I gave him a hail, and he presented himself with a courteous 'Sir?'

'Oh, Jeeves,' I said, 'I hope I'm not interrupting you when you were curled up with your Spinoza's Ethics or whatever it is,

but I wonder if you could spare me a moment of your valuable
time?'

'Certainly, sir.'

'A problem has arisen in the life of a friend of mine who shall
be nameless, and I want your advice. I must begin by saying
that it's one of those delicate problems where not only my
friend must be nameless but all the other members of the per-
sonnel. In other words, I can't mention names. You see what I
mean?'

'I understand you perfectly, sir. You would prefer to term
the protagonists A and B.'

'Or North and South?'

'A and B is more customary, sir.'

'Just as you say. Well, A is male, B female. You follow me so
far?'

'You have been lucidity itself, sir.'

'And owing to ... what's that something of circumstances
you hear people talking about? Cats enter into it, if I remember
rightly.'

'Would concatenation be the word for which you are groping?'

'That's it. Owing to a concatenation of circumstances B has
got it into her nut A's in love with her. But he isn't. Still following?'

'Yes, sir.'

I had to pause here for a moment to marshal my thoughts.
Having done so, I proceeded.

'Now until quite recently B was engaged to — '

'Shall we call him C, sir?'

'Caesar's as good a name as any, I suppose. Well, as I was
saying, until quite recently B was engaged to Caesar and A
hadn't a worry in the world. But now there has been a rift
within the lute, the fixture has been scratched and B is talking
freely of teaming up with A, and what I want you to bend your
brain to is the problem of how A can oil out of it. Don't get the
idea that it's simple, because A is what is known as a preux
chevalier, and this hampers him. I mean when B comes to him
and say "A, I will be yours," he can't just reply "You will, will
you? That's what *you* think". He has his code, and the code
rules that he must kid her along and accept the situation. And

frankly, Jeeves, he would rather be dead in a ditch. So there you are. The facts are before you. Anything stirring?'

'Yes, sir.'

I was astounded. Experience has taught me that he generally knows all the answers, but this was certainly quick service.

'Say on, Jeeves. I'm all agog.'

'Obviously, sir, B's matrimonial plans would be rendered null and void if A were to inform her that his affections were engaged elsewhere.'

'But they aren't.'

'It would be necessary merely to convey the impression that such was the case.'

I began to see what he was driving at.

'You mean if I — or, rather, A — were to produce some female and have her assert that she was betrothed to me — or I should say him — the peril would be averted?'

'Precisely, sir.'

I mused.

'It's a thought,' I agreed, 'but there's the dickens of a snag — viz, how to get hold of the party of the second part. You can't rush about London asking girls to pretend they're engaged to you. At least, I supose you can, but it would be quite a nervous strain.'

'That, sir, *is* the difficulty.'

'You haven't an alternative plan to suggest?'

'I fear not, sir.'

I confess I was baffled, but it's pretty generally recognised at the Drones and elsewhere that while you can sometimes baffle Bertram Wooster for the nonce, he rarely stays baffled long. I happened to run into Catsmeat Potter-Pirbright at the Drones that night, and I suddenly saw how the snag to which I had alluded could be got around.

Catsmeat is on the stage and now in considerable demand for what are called juvenile roles, but in his early days he had been obliged, like all young hams, to go from agent to agent seeking employment — or trying to get a shop, as I believe the technical term is, and he was telling me anecdotes about them after dinner. And it struck me like blow in the midriff that if you wanted a girl to exhibit as your fiancée, a theatrical agent was the very man to help you out. Such a bloke would be in an admirable position to supply some resting artiste who would be glad to sit in on an innocent deception in return for a moderate fee.

Catsmeat had told me where these fauna were to be found. The Charing Cross Road is apparently where most of them hang out, and on the following morning I might have been observed entering the premises of Jas Waterbury on the top floor of a building about half way up that thoroughfare.

The reason my choice had fallen on Jas was not that I had heard glowing reports of him from every side, it was simply because all the other places I had tried had been full of guys and dolls standing bumper to bumper and it hadn't seemed worth while waiting. Entering *chez* Waterbury I found his outer office completely empty. It was as if he had parted company with the human herd.

It was possible, of course, that he had stepped across the road for a quick one, but it was also possible that he was lurking behind the door labelled Private, so I rapped on it. I hadn't expected anything to start into life, but I was wrong. A head popped out.

I've seen heads that were more of a feast for the eye. It was what I would describe as a greasy head. Its summit was moist with hair oil and the face, too, suggested that its proprietor after the morning shave had thought fit to rub his cheeks with butter. But I'm a broad-minded man and I had no objection to him being greasy, if he liked being greasy. Possibly, I felt, if I had had the privilege of meeting Kenneth Molyneux, Malcolm McCullen, Edmund Ogilvy, and Horace Furnival, the other theatrical agents I had visited, I would have found them greasy, too. It may be that all theatrical agents are. I made a mental note to ask Catsment Potter-Pirbright about this.

'Oh, hullo, cocky,' said this oleaginous character, speaking thickly, for he was making an early lunch on what looked like a ham sandwich. 'Something I can do for you?'

'Jas Waterbury?'

'That's me. You want a shop?'

'I want a girl.'

'Don't we all? What's your line? Are you running a touring company?'

'No, it's more like amateur theatricals?'

'Oh, those? Well, let's have the inside story.'

I had told myself that it would be embarrassing confiding one's intimate private affairs to a theatrical agent, and it was embarrassing, but I stiffened the upper lip and had at it, and as my narrative proceeded it was borne in upon me that I had sized up Jas Waterbury all wrong. Misled by his appearance, I had assumed him to be one of those greasy birds who would be slow on the uptake and unable to get help to the finer points. He proved to be both quick and intelligent. He punctuated my remarks with understanding nods, and when I had finished said I had come to the right man, for he had a niece called Trixie who would fill the bill to my complete satisfaction. The whole project, he said, was right up Trixie's street. If I placed myself in her hands, he added, the act must infallibly be a smash hit.

It sounded good, but I pursed my lips a bit dubiously. I was asking myself if an uncle's love might not have made him give the above Trixie too enthusiastic a build-up.

'You're sure,' I said, 'that this niece of yours would be equal to this rather testing job? It calls for considerable histrionic skill. Can she make her role convincing?'

'She'll smother you with burning kisses, if that's what you're worrying about.'

'What I had in mind was more the dialogue. We don't want her blowing up in her lines. Don't you think we ought to get a seasoned professional?'

'That's just what Trixie is. Been playing Fairy Queens in panto for years. Never got a shop in London owing to jealousy in high places, but ask them in Leeds and Wigan what they think of her. Ask them in Hull. Ask them in Huddersfield.'

I said I would, always provided I happened to come across them, and he carried on in a sort of ecstasy.

' "This buxom belle" — *Leeds Evening Chronicle*. "A talented bit of all right" — *Hull Daily News*. "Beauty and dignity combined" — *Wigan Intelligencer*. Don't you fret yourself, cocky, Trix'll give you your money's worth. And talking of that, how much does the part pay?'

'I was thinking of a fiver.'

'Make it ten.'

'Right ho.'

'Or, rather, fifteen. That way you'll get every ounce of zest and co-operation.'

I was in no mood to haggle. Aunt Dahlia had rung up while I was breakfasting to tell me that Honoria Glossop had told her that she would be looking in on me at four o'clock, and it was imperative that the reception committee be on hand to greet her. I dished out the fifteen quid and asked how soon he could get hold of his niece, as time was of the essence. He said her services would be at my disposal well ahead of zero hour, and I said Fine.

'Give me a ring when it's all set,' I said. 'I'll be lunching at the Drones Club.'

This seemed to interest him quite a bit.

'Drones Club, eh? You a member there? I've got some good friends at the Drones Club. You know a Mr Widgeon?'

'Freddie Widgeon? Yes, very well.'

'And Mr. Prosser?'

'Yes, I know Oofy Prosser.'

'Give them my best, if you see them. Nice lads, both. And now you can trot along and feed your face without a care in the world. I'll have contacted Trixie before you're half way through your fish and chips.'

And I was called to the phone while having the after-luncheon coffee in the smoking-room. It was, as I had anticipated, Jas Waterbury.

'That you, cocky?'

I said it was, and he said everything was under control. Trixie had been contacted and would be up and doing with a heart for any fate in good time for the rise of the curtain. What, he asked, was the address they were to come to, and I told him and he said they would be there at a quarter to four without fail. So that was all fixed, and I was full of kindly feelings towards Jas Waterbury as I made my way back to the smoking-room. He was a man whom I would have hesitated to invite to come with me on a long walking tour and I still felt that he would have been well advised to go easier on the grease as regarded both his hair and his person, but there was no getting away from it that if circumstances rendered it necessary for you to plot plots, he was the ideal fellow to plot them with.

During my absence from the smoking-room Catsmeat Potter-

Pirbright had taken the chair next to mine, and I lost no time in sounding him out on the subject of Jas Waterbury.

'You remember you were telling me about theatrical agents, Catsmeat. Did you ever happen to come across one called Waterbury?'

He pondered awhile.

'The name seems vaguely familiar. What does he look like?'

'Nothing on earth.'

'That doesn't place him. All theatrical agents look like nothing on earth. But it's odd that I seem to know the name. Waterbury? Waterbury? Ha! Is he a greasy bird?'

'Very greasy.'

'And is his first name Jas?'

'That's right.'

'Then I know the chap you mean. I never met him myself — I doubt if he was going at the time when I was hoofing it from agent to agent — but I've heard of him from Freddie Widgeon and Oofy Prosser.'

'Yes, he said they were friends of his.'

'He'd revise that view if he could listen to them talking about him. Oofy in particular. Jas Waterbury once chiselled him out of two thousand pounds.'

I was amazed.

'He chiselled *Oofy* out of two thousand pounds?' I gasped, wondering if I could believe my e. Oofy is the Drones Club millionaire, but it is well known that it's practically impossible to extract as much as five bob from him without using chloroform and a forceps. Dozens have tried it and failed.

'That's what Freddie Widgeon told me. Freddie says that once Jas Waterbury enters your life, you can kiss at least a portion of your holdings goodbye. Has he taken anything off you?'

'Fifteen quid.'

'You're lucky it wasn't fifteen hundred.'

If you're saying to yourself that these words of Catsmeat's must have left me uneasy and apprehensive, you are correct to the last drop. A quarter to four found me pacing the Wooster carpet with furrowed brow. If it had been merely a matter of this grease-coated theatrical agent tapping Freddie Widgeon for a couple of bob, it would have been different. A child can tap Freddie. But when it came to him parting Oofy Prosser, a man in whose wallet moths nest and raise large families, from a colossal sum like two thousand pounds, the brain reeled and one sought in vain for an explanation. Yet so it was. Catsmeat said it was impossible to get the full story, because every time Jas's name was mentioned Oofy just turned purple and spluttered, but the stark fact remained that Jas's bank balance was that amount up and Oofy's that amount down, and it made me feel like a fellow in a novel of suspense who suddenly realises that he's up against an Octopus of Crime and hasn't the foggiest how he's going to avoid the menacing tentacles.

But it wasn't long before Reason returned to its throne and I saw that I'd been alarming myself unnecessarily. Nothing like that was going to happen to me. It might be that Jas Waterbury would have a shot at luring me into some business venture with the ultimate aim of leaving me holding the baby, but if he did he would find himself stymied by a firm nolle prosequi, so, to cut a long story s, by the time the front door bell rang Bertram was himself again.

I answered the bell, for it was Jeeves's afternoon off. Once a week he downs tools and goes off to play Bridge at the Junior Ganymede. I opened the door and Jas and his niece came in, and I stood gaping dumbly. For an instant, you might say I was spellbound.

Not having attended the performance of a pantomime since fairly early childhood, I had forgotten how substantial Fairy Queens were, and the sight of Trixie Waterbury was like a blow from a blunt instrument. A glance was enough to tell me why the dramatic critic of the *Leeds Evening Chronicle* had called her buxom. She stood about five feet nine in her short French vamps and bulged in every direction. Also the flashing eyes and the gleaming teeth. It was some moment before I was able to say Good Afternoon.

'Afternoon,' said Jas Waterbury. He looked about him approvingly. 'Nice little place you've got here. Costs a packet to keep up, I'll bet. This is Mr. Wooster, Trixie. You call him Bertie.'

The Fairy Queen said wouldn't 'sweetie-pie' be better, and

Jas Waterbury told her with a good deal of enthusiasm that she was quite right.

'Much more box office,' he agreed. 'Didn't I say she would be right for the part, cocky? You can rely on her to give a smooth West End performance. When do you expect your lady friend?'

'Any moment now.'

'Then we'd better be dressing the stage. Discovered, you sitting in that chair there with Trixie on your lap.'

'What!'

He seemed to sense the consternation in my voice, for he frowned a little under the grease.

'We're all working for the good of the show,' he reminded me austerely. 'You want the scene to carry conviction, and there's nothing like a sight gag.'

I could see there was much in what he said. This was not a time for half measures. I sat down. I don't say I sat blithely, but I sat, and Wigan's favourite Fairy Queen descended on my lap with a bump that made the stout chair tremble like an aspen. And scarcely had she started to nestle when the door bell rang.

'Curtain going up,' said Jas Waterbury. 'Let's have that passionate embrace, Trixie, and make it good.'

She made it good, and I felt like a Swiss mountaineer engulfed by an avalanche smelling of patchouli. Jas Waterbury flung wide the gates, and who should come in but Blair Eggleston, the last caller I was expecting.

He stood goggling. I sat goggling. Jas Waterbury goggled, too. One could understand how he was feeling. Anticipating the entrance of the female star and observing coming on left centre a character who wasn't a member of the cast at all, he was pardonably disconcerted. No impresario likes that sort of thing.

I was first to speak. After all, I was the host and it was for me to get the conversation going.

'Oh, hullo, Eggleston,' I said. 'Come along in. I don't think you've met Mr. Waterbury, have you, Mr. Eggleston, Mr. Jas Waterbury. And his niece Miss Trixie Waterbury, my fiancée.'

'Your *what*?'

'Fiancée. Betrothed. Affianced.'

'Good Lord!'

Jas Waterbury appeared to be feeling that as the act had

been shot to pieces like this, there was no sense in hanging around.

'Well, Trix,' he said, 'your Bertie'll be wanting to talk to his gentleman friend, so give him a kiss and we'll be getting along. Pleased to have met you, Mr. What-is-it,' and with a greasy smile he led the Fairy Queen from the room.

Blair Eggleston seemed still at a loss. He looked at the door through which they had passed as if asking himself if he had really seen what he thought he had seen, then turned to me with the air of one who intends to demand an explanation.

'What's all this, Wooster?'

'What's all what, Eggleston? Be more explicit.'

'Who on earth is that female?'

'Weren't you listening? My fiancée.'

'You're really engaged to her?'

'That's right.'

'Who is she?'

'She plays Fairy Queens in pantomime. Not in London owing to jealousy in high places, but they think a lot of her in Leeds, Wigan, Hull, and Huddersfield. The critic of the *Hull Daily News* describes her as a talented bit of all right.'

He was silent for a space, appearing to be turning this over in his mind. Then he spoke in the frank, forthright and fearless way these modern novelists have.

'She looks like a hippopotamus.'

I conceded this.

'There is a resemblance, perhaps. I suppose Fairy Queens have to be stoutish if they are to keep faith with their public in towns like Leeds and Huddersfield. Those audiences up North wants lots for their money.'

'And she exudes a horrible scent which I am unable at the moment to identify.'

'Patchouli. Yes, I noticed that.'

He mused again.

'I can't get over you being engaged to her.'

'Well, I am.'

'It's official?'

'Absolutely.'

'Well, this will be great news for Honoria.'

I didn't get his drift.

'For Honoria?'

'Yes. It will relieve her mind. She was very worried about you, poor child. That's why I'm here. I came to break it to you that she can never be yours. She's going to marry me.'

I stared at him. My first impression was that even though the hour was only about four-thirty he was under the influence of alcoholic stimulants.

'But I learned from a usually reliable source that that was all off.'

'It was, but now it's on again. We have had a complete reconciliation.'

'Well, fancy that!'

'And she shrank from coming and telling you herself. She said she couldn't bear to see the awful dumb agony in your eyes. When I tell her you're engaged, she'll go singing about the West End of London, not only because of the relief of knowing that she hasn't wrecked your life but because she'll be feeling what a merciful escape she's had. Just imagine being married to you! It doesn't bear thinking of. Well, I'll be going along and telling her the good news,' he said, and took his departure.

A moment later the bell rang. I opened the door and found him on the mat.

'What,' he asked, 'was that name again?'

'Name?'

'Your fiancée's.'

'Trixie Waterbury.'

'Good God!' he said, and pushed off. And I returned to the reverie he had interrupted.

There was a time when if somebody had come to me and said 'Mr. Wooster, I have been commissioned by a prominent firm of publishers to write your biography and I need some intimate stuff which only you can supply. Looking back, what would you consider the high spot of your career?' I would have had no difficulty in slipping him the info. It occurred, I would have replied, in my fourteenth year when I was a resident pupil at Malvern House, Bramley-on-Sea, the private school conducted by the prince of stinkers, Aubrey Upjohn, MA. He had told me to present myself in his study on the following morning, which always meant six of the juiciest with a cane that bit like a serpent and stung like an adder, and blowed if when morning came, I wasn't all over pink spots. I had contracted measles and the painful interview was of course postponed *sine die*, as the expression is.

That had always been my supreme moment. Only now was I experiencing to an even greater extent the feeling of quiet happiness which comes to you when you've outsmarted the powers of darkness. I felt as if a great weight had been lifted off me. Well, it had of course in one sense, for the Fairy Queen must have clocked in at fully a hundred and sixty pounds ringside, but what I mean is that a colossal burden had been removed from the Wooster soul. It was as though the storm clouds had called it a day and the sun come smiling through.

The only thing that kept the moment from being absolutely perfect was that Jeeves was not there to share my hour of triumph. I toyed with the idea of ringing him up at the Junior Ganymede, but I didn't want to interrupt him when he was probably in the act of doubling six no trumps.

The thought of Aunt Dahlia presented itself. She of all people should be the one to hear the good news, for she was very fond of Roddy Glossop and had shown herself deeply concerned when informed of his in-the-soup-ness. Furthermore, she could scarcely not be relieved to learn that a loved nephew had escaped the fate that is worse than death — viz. marrying Honoria. It was true that my firm refusal to play Santa Claus at her children's party must still be rankling, if that's the word, but at our last meeting I had found her far less incandescent than she had been, so there was reason to suppose that if I looked in on her now I should get a cordial reception. Well, not absolutely cordial, perhaps, but something near enough to it. So I left a note for Jeeves saying where I'd gone and hared off to her address in a swift taxi.

It was as I had anticipated. I don't say her face lit up when she saw me, but she didn't throw her Perry Mason at me and she called me no new names, and after I had told my story she was all joviality and enthusiasm. We were saying what a wonderful Christmas present the latest development would be for Pop Glossop and speculating as to what it would feel like being married to his daughter Honoria and, for the matter of that, being married to Blair Eggleston, and we had just agreed that both Honoria and Blair had it coming to them, when the telephone rang. The instrument was on a table near her chair, and she reached for it.

'Hullo?' she boomed. 'Who?' Or rather, WHO, for when at the telephone her vocal delivery is always of much the same calibre as it used to be on the hunting field. She handed me the receiver. 'One of your foul friends wants you. Says his name's Waterbury.'

Jas Waterbury, placed in communication with self, seemed perplexed. In rather an awed voice he asked:

'Where are you, cocky? At the Zoo?'

'I don't follow you, Jas Waterbury.'

'A lion just roared at me.'

'Oh, that was my aunt.'

'Sooner yours than mine. I thought the top of my head had come off.'

'She has a robust voice.'

'I'll say she has. Well, cully, I'm sorry I had to disturb her at feeding time, but I thought you'd like to know that Trix and I have been talking it over and we both think a simple wedding at the registrar's would be best. No need for a lot of fuss and expense. And she says she'd like Brighton for the honeymoon. She's always been fond of Brighton.'

I was at something of a loss to know what on earth he was talking about, but reading between the lines I gathered that the Fairy Queen was thinking of getting married. I asked if this was so, and he chuckled greasily.

'Always kidding, Bertie. You will have your joke. If you don't know she's going to get married, who does?'

'I haven't a notion. Who to?'

'Why, you, of course. Didn't you introduce her to your gentleman friend as your fiancée?'

I lost no time in putting him straight.

'But that was just a ruse. Surely you explained it to her?'

'Explained what?'

'That I just wanted her to pretend that we were engaged.'

'What an extraordinary idea. What would I have done that for?'

'Fifteen quid.'

'I don't remember any fifteen quid. As I recall it, you came to me and told me you'd seen Trixie as the Fairy Queen in Cinderella at the Wigan Hippodrome and fallen in love with her at first sight, as so many young fellows have done. You had found out somehow that she was my niece and you asked me to bring her to your address. And the moment we came in I could see the love light in your eyes, and the love light was in her eyes, too, and it wasn't five minutes after that that you'd got her on your lap and there you were, as snug as two bugs in a rug. Just a case of love at first sight, and I don't mind telling you it touched me. I like to see the young folks getting together in Springtime. Not that it's Springtime now, but the principle's the same.'

At this point Aunt Dahlia, who had been simmering gently, intervened to call me a derogatory name and ask what the hell was going on. I waved her down with an imperious hand. I needed every ounce of concentration to cope with this mis-understanding which seemed to have arisen.

'You're talking through your hat, Jas Waterbury.'

'Who, me?'

'Yes, you. You've got your facts all wrong.'

'You think so, do you?'

'I do, and I will trouble you to break it to Miss Waterbury that those wedding bells will not ring out.'

'That's what I was telling you. Trixie wants it to be at the registrar's.'

'Well, that registrar won't ring out, either.'

He said I amazed him.

'You don't want to marry Trixie?'

'I wouldn't marry her with a ten foot pole.'

An astonished 'Lord love a duck' came over the wire.

'If that isn't the most remarkable coincidence,' he said. 'Those were the very words Mr. Prosser used when refusing to marry another niece of mine after announcing his betrothal before witnesses, same as you did. Shows what a small world it is. I asked him if he hadn't ever heard of breach of promise cases, and he shook visibly and swallowed once or twice. Then he looked me in the eye and said "How much?" I didn't get his meaning at first, and then it suddenly flashed on me. "Oh, you mean you want to break the engagement," I said, "and feel it's your duty as a gentleman to see that the poor girl gets her bit of heart balm," I said. "Well, it'll have to be something substantial," I said, "because there's her despair and desolation to be taken into account." So we talked it over and eventually settled on two thousand quid, and that's what I'd advise in your case. I think I can talk Trixie into accepting that. Nothing, mind you, can ever make life anything but a dreary desert for her after losing you, but two thousand quid would help.'

'BERTIE!' said Aunt Dahlia.

'Ah,' said Jas Waterbury, 'there's that lion again. Well, I'll leave you to think it over. I'll come and see you tomorrow and get your decision, and if you feel that you don't like writing that cheque, I'll ask a friend of mine to try what he can do to persuade you. He's an all-in wrestler of the name of Porky Jupp. I used to manage him at one time. He's retired now because he broke a fellow's spine and for some reason that gave him a distaste of the game. But he's still in wonderful condition. You ought to see him crack Brazil nuts with his fingers. He thinks the world of me and there's nothing he wouldn't do for me. Suppose, for instance, somebody had done me down in a business transaction, Porky would spring to the task of plucking him limb from limb like some innocent little child doing She-loves-me-not with a daisy. Good night, good night,' said Jas Waterbury, and rang off.

I would have preferred, of course, after this exceedingly unpleasant conversation to have gone off into a quiet corner somewhere and sat there with my head between my hands, reviewing the situation from every angle, but Aunt Dahlia was now making her desire for explanatory notes so manifest that I had to give her my attention. In a broken voice I supplied her with the facts and was surprised and touched to find her sympathetic and understanding. It's often this way with the female sex. They put you through it in no uncertain manner if you won't see eye to eye with them in the matter — to take an instance at random — of disguising yourself in white whiskers and stomach padding, but if they see you are really up against it, their hearts melt, rancour is forgotten and they do all they can to give you a shot in the arm. It was so with the aged relative. Having expressed the opinion that I was the king of the fatheads and ought never to be allowed out without a nurse, she continued in gentler strain.

'But after all you are my brother's son whom I frequently dandled on my knee as a baby, and a subhuman baby you were if ever I saw one, though I suppose you were to be pitied rather then censured if you looked like a cross between a poached egg and a ventriloquist's dummy, so I can't let you sink in the soup without a trace. I must rally round and lend a hand.'

'Well, thanks, old flesh and blood. Awfully decent of you to want to assist. But what can you do?'

'Nothing by myself, perhaps, but I can confer with Jeeves and between us we ought to think of something. Ring him up and tell him to come here at once.'

'He won't be home yet. He's playing Bridge at his club.'

'Give him a buzz, anyway.'

I did so, and was surprised when I heard a measured voice say 'Mr. Wooster's residence'.

'Why, hullo, Jeeves,' I said, 'I didn't expect you to be home so early.'

'I left in advance of my usual hour, sir. I did not find my Bridge game enjoyable.'

'Bad cards?'

'No, sir, the hands dealt to me were uniformly satisfactory, but I was twice taken out of business doubles, and I had not the heart to continue.'

'Too bad. So you're at a loose end at the moment?'

'Yes, sir.'

'Then will you hasten to Aunt Dahlia's place? You are sorely needed.'

'Very good, sir.'

'Is he coming?' said Aunt Dahlia.

'Like the wind. Just looking for his bowler hat.'

'Then you pop off.'

'You don't want me for the conference?'

'No.'

'Three heads are better than two,' I argued.

'Not if one of them is solid ivory from the neck up,' said the aged relative, reverting to something more like her customary form.

I slept fitfully that night, my slumbers much disturbed by

dreams of being chased across country by a pack of Fairy Queens with Jas Waterbury galloping after them shouting Yoicks and Tally ho. It was past eleven when I presented myself at the breakfast table.

'I take it, Jeeves,' I said as I started to pick at a moody fried egg, 'that Aunt Dahlia has told you all?'

'Yes, sir, Mrs. Travers was most informative.'

Well, that was a relief in a way, because all that secrecy and A-and-B stuff is always a strain.

'Disaster looms, wouldn't you say?'

'Certainly your predicament is one of some gravity, sir.'

'I can't face a breach of promise action with a crowded court giving me the horse's laugh and the jury mulcting ... Is it mulcting?'

'Yes, sir, you are quite correct.'

'And the jury mulcting me in heavy damages. I wouldn't be able to show my face in the Drones again.'

'The publicity would certainly not be agreeable, sir.'

'On the other hand, I thoroughly dislike the idea of paying Jas Waterbury two thousand pounds.'

'I can appreciate your dilemma, sir.'

'But perhaps you have already thought of some terrific scheme for foiling Jas and bringing his greasy hairs in sorrow to the grave. What do you plan to do when he calls?'

'I shall attempt to reason with him, sir.'

The heart turned to lead in the bosom. I suppose I've become so used to having Jeeves wave his magic wand and knock the stuffing out of the stickiest crises that I expect him to produce something brilliant from the hat every time, and though never at my brightest at breakfast I could see that what he was proposing to do was far from being what Jas Waterbury would have called box office. Reason with him, forsooth! To reason successfully with that king of the twisters one would need brass knucks and a stocking full of sand. There was reproach in my voice as I asked him if that was the best he could do.

'You do not think highly of the idea, sir?'

'Well, I don't want to hurt your feelings — '

'Not at all, sir.'

' — but I wouldn't call it one of your top thoughts.'

'I am sorry, sir. Nevertheless — '

I leaped from the table, the fried egg frozen on my lips. The front door bell had given tongue. I don't know if my eyes actually rolled as I gazed at Jeeves, but I should think it extremely likely, for the sound had got in amongst me like the touching off an ounce or so of trinitrotoluene.

'There he is!'

'Presumably, sir.'

'I can't face him as early in the morning as this.'

'One appreciates your emotion, sir. It might be advisable if you were to conceal yourself while I conduct the negotiations. Behind the piano suggests itself as a suitable locale.'

'How right you are, Jeeves!'

To say that I found it comfortable behind the piano would be to give my public a totally erroneous impression, but I secured privacy, and privacy was just what I was after. The facilities, too, for keeping in touch with what was going on in the great world outside were excellent. I heard the door opening and then Jas Waterbury's voice.

'Morning, cocky.'

'Good morning, sir.'

'Wooster in?'

'No, sir, he has just stepped out.'

'That's odd. He was expecting me.'

'You are Mr. Waterbury?'

'That's me. Where's he gone?'

'I think it was Mr. Wooster's intention to visit his pawnbroker, sir.'

'What!'

'He mentioned something to me about doing so. He said he hoped to raise, as he expressed it, a few pounds on his watch.'

'You're kidding! What's he want to pop his watch for?'

'His means are extremely straitened.'

There was what I've heard called a pregnant silence. I took it that Jas Waterbury was taking time off to allow this to sink in. I wished I could have joined in the conversation, for I would have liked to say 'Jeeves, you are on the right lines' and offer him an apology for ever having doubted him. I might have known that when he said he was going to reason with Jas he had the ace up his sleeve which makes all the difference.

It was some little time before Jas Waterbury spoke, and

when he did his voice had a sort of tremolo in it, as if he'd begun to realise that life wasn't the thing of roses and sunshine he'd been thinking it. I knew how he must be feeling. There is no anguish like that of the man who, supposing that he has found the pot of gold behind the rainbow, suddenly learns from an authoritative source that he hasn't, if you know what I mean. To him until now Bertram Wooster had been a careless scatterer of fifteen quids, a thing you can't do if you haven't a solid bank balance behind you, and to have him presented to him as a popper of watches must have made the iron enter into his soul, if he had one. He spoke as if stunned.

'But what about this place of his?'

'Sir?'

'You don't get a Park Lane flat for nothing.'

'No indeed, sir.'

'Let alone a vally.'

'Sir?'

'You're a vally, aren't you?'

'No, sir. I was at one time a gentleman's personal gentleman, but at the moment I am not employed in that capacity. I represent Messrs. Alsopp and Wilson, wine merchants, goods supplied to the value of three hundred and four pounds, fifteen shillings and eightpence, a bill which Mr. Wooster finds it far beyond his fiscal means to settle. I am what is technically known as the man in possession.'

A hoarse 'Gorblimey' burst from Jas's lips. I thought it rather creditable of him that he did not say anything stronger.

'You mean you're a broker's man?'

'Precisely, sir. I am sorry to say I have come down in the world and my present situation was the only one I could secure. But while not what I have been accustomed to, it has its compensations. Mr. Wooster is a very agreeable young gentleman and takes my intrusion in an amiable spirit. We have long and interesting conversations, and in the course of these he has confided his financial position to me. It appears that he is entirely dependent on the bounty of his aunt, a Mrs. Travers, a lady of uncertain temper who has several times threatened unless he curbs his extravagance to cancel his allowance and send him to Canada to subsist on a small monthly remittance. She is of course under the impression that I am Mr. Wooster's personal attendant. Should she learn of my official status, I do not like to envisage the outcome, though if I may venture on a pleasantry it would be a case of outgo rather than outcome for Mr. Wooster.'

There was another pregnant s, occupied, I should imagine, by Jas Waterbury in wiping his brow, which one presumes had by this time become wet with honest sweat.

Finally he once more said 'Gorblimey'.

Whether or not he would have amplified the remark I cannot say, for his words, if he had intended uttering any, were dashed from his lips. There was a sound like a mighty rushing wind and a loud snort informed me that Aunt Dahlia was with us. In letting Jas Waterbury in, Jeeves must have omitted to close the front door.

'Jeeves,' she boomed, 'can you look me in the face?'

'Certainly, madam, if you wish.'

'Well, I'm surprised you can. You must have the gall of an Army mule. I've just found out that you're a broker's man in valet's clothing. Can you deny it?'

'No, madam. I represent Messrs. Alsopp and Wilson, wines, spirits and liqueurs supplied to the value of three hundred and four pounds fifteen shillings and eightpence.'

The piano behind which I cowered hummed like a dynamo as the aged relative unshipped a second snort.

'Good God! What does young Bertie do — bathe in the stuff? Three hundred and four pounds fifteen shillings and eight-pence! Probably owes as much, too, in a dozen other places. And in the red to that extent he's planning, I hear, to marry the fat woman in a circus.'

'A portrayer of Fairy Queens in pantomime, madam.'

'Just as bad. Blair Eggleston says she looks like a hip-popotamus.'

'I couldn't see him, of course, but I imagine Jas Waterbury drew himself to his full height at this description of the loved niece, for his voice when he spoke was stiff and offended.

'That's my Trixie you're talking about, and he's going to marry her or else get sued for breach of promise.'

It's just a guess, but I think Aunt Dahlia must have drawn herself to her full height, too.

'Well, she'll have to go to Canada to bring her action,' she thundered, 'because that's where Bertie Wooster'll be off to on the next boat, and when he's there he won't have money to fritter away on breach of promise cases. It'll be as much as he can manage to keep body and soul together on what I'm going to allow him. If he gets a meat meal every third day, he'll be lucky. You tell that Trixie of yours to forget Bertie and go and marry the Demon King.'

Experience has taught me that except in vital matters like playing Santa Claus at children's parties it's impossible to defy Aunt Dahlia, and apparently Jas Waterbury realised this, for a moment later I heard the front door slam. He had gone without a cry.

'So that's that,' said Aunt Dahlia. 'These emotional scenes take it out of one, Jeeves. Can you get me a drop of something sustaining?'

'Certainly, madam.'

'How was I? All right?'

'Superb, madam.'

'I think I was in good voice.'

'Very sonorous, madam.'

'Well, it's nice to think our efforts were crowned with success. This will relieve young Bertie's mind. I use the word mind loosely. When do you expect him back?'

'Mr. Wooster is in residence, madam. Shrinking from confronting Mr. Waterbury, he prudently concealed himself. You will find him behind the piano.'

I was already emerging, and my first act was to pay them both a marked tribute. Jeeves accepted it gracefully, Aunt Dahlia with another of those snorts. Having snorted, she spoke as follows.

'Easy enough for you to hand out the soft soap, but what I'd like to see is less guff and more action. If you were really grateful, you would play Santa Claus at my Christmas party.'

I could see her point. It was well taken. I clenched the hands, I set the jaw. I made the great decision.

'Very well, aged relative.'

'You will?'

'I will.'

'That's my boy. What's there to be afraid of? The worst those kids will do is rub chocolate eclairs on your whiskers.'

'Chocolate eclairs?' I said in a low voice.

'Or strawberry jam. It's a tribal custom. Pay no attention, by the way, to stories you may have heard of them setting fire to the curate's beard last year. It was purely accidental.'

I had begun to go into my aspen act, when Jeeves spoke.

'Pardon me, madam.'

'Yes Jeeves?'

'If I might offer the suggestion, I think that perhaps a maturer artist than Mr. Wooster would give a more convincing performance.'

'Don't tell me you're thinking of volunteering?'

'No, madam. The artist I had in mind was Sir Roderick Glossop. Sir Roderick has a fine presence and a somewhat deeper voice than Mr. Wooster. His Ho-ho-ho would be more dramatically effective, and I am sure that if you approached him, you could persuade him to undertake the role.'

'Considering,' I said, putting in my oar, 'that he is always blacking up his face with burned cork.'

'Precisely, sir. This will make a nice change.'

Aunt Dahlia pondered.

'I believe you're right, Jeeves,' she said at length. 'It's tough on those children, for it means robbing them of the biggest laugh they've ever had, but they can't expect life to be one round of pleasure. Well, I don't think I'll have that drink after all. It's a bit early.'

She buzzed off, and I turned to Jeeves, deeply moved. He had saved me from an ordeal at the thought of which the flesh crept, for I hadn't believed for a moment the aged r's story of the blaze in the curate's beard having been an accident. The young element had probably sat up nights planning it out.

'Jeeves,' I said, 'you were saying something not long ago about going to Florida after Christmas.'

'It was merely a suggestion, sir.'

'You want to catch a tarpon, do you not?'

'I confess that it is my ambition, sir.'

I sighed. It wasn't so much that it pained me to think of some tarpon, perhaps a wife and mother, being jerked from the society of its loved ones on the end of a hook. What gashed me like a knife was the thought of missing the Drones Club Darts

Tournament, for which I would have been a snip this year. But what would you? I fought down my regret.

'Then will you be booking the tickets.'

'Very good, sir.'

I struck a graver note.

'Heaven help the tarpon that tries to pit its feeble cunning against you, Jeeves,' I said. 'Its efforts will be bootless.'

* 2 *

Sticky Wicket at Blandings

It was a beautiful afternoon. They sky was blue, the sun yellow, butterflies flitted, birds tooted, bees buzzed and, to cut a long story short, all Nature smiled. But on Lord Emsworth's younger son Freddie Threepwood, as he sat in his sports model car at the front door of Blandings Castle, a fine Alsatian dog at his side, these excellent weather conditions made little impression. He was thinking of dog biscuits.

Freddie was only an occasional visitor at the castle these days. Some years before, he had married the charming daughter of Mr. Donaldson of Donaldson's Dog Joy, the organisation whose aim it is to keep the American dog one hundred per cent red-blooded by supplying it with wholesome and nourishing biscuits and had gone off to Long Island City, U.S.A. to work for the firm. He was in England now because his father-in-law, anxious to extend Dog Joy's sphere of influence, had sent him back there to see what he could do in the way of increasing sales in the island kingdom. Aggie, his wife, had accompanied him, but after a week or so had found life at Blandings too quiet for her and had left for the French Riviera. The arrangement was that at the conclusion of his English campaign Freddie should join her there.

He was drying his left ear, on which the Alsatian had just bestowed a moist caress, when there came down the front steps

a small, dapper elderly gentleman with a black-rimmed
monocle in his eye. This was that notable figure of London's
Bohemia, his Uncle Galahad, at whom the world of the theatre,
the racehorse and the livelier type of restaurant had been pointing with pride for years. He greeted him cordially. To his
sisters Constance, Julia, Dora, and Hermione Gally might be a
blot on the escutcheon, but in Freddie he excited only admiration. He considered him a man of infinite resources and saga-
city, as indeed he was.

'Well, young Freddie,' said Gally. 'Where are you off to with
that dog?'

'I'm taking him to the Fanshawes.'

'At Marling Hall? That's where that pretty girl I met you
with the other day lives, isn't it?'

'That's right. Valerie Fanshawe. Her father's the local
Master of Hounds. And you know what that means.'

'What does it mean?'

'That he's the managing director of more dogs than you
could shake a stick at, each dog requiring the daily biscuit. And
what could be better for them than Donaldson's Dog Joy, containing as it does all the essential vitamins?'

'You're going to sell him dog biscuits?'

'I don't see how I can miss. Valerie is the apple of his eye, to
whom he can deny nothing. She covets this Alsatian and says if
I'll give it to her, she'll see that the old man comes through
with a substantial order. I'm about to deliver it F.O.B.'

'But, my good Freddie, that dog is Aggie's dog. She'll go up
in flames.'

'Oh, that's all right. I've budgeted for that. I have my story
all set and ready. I shall tell her it died and I'll get her another
just as good. That'll fix Aggie. But I mustn't sit here chewing
the fat with you. I must be up and about and off and away.
See you later,' said Freddie, and disappeared in a cloud of
smoke.

He left Gally pursing his lips. A lifetime spent in the society
of bookies, racecourse touts and skittle sharps had made him
singularly broadminded, but he could not regard these tactics
with approval. Shaking his head, he went back into the house
and in the hall encountered Beach, the castle butler. Beach was
wheezing a little, for he had been hurrying, and he was no

longer the streamlined young butler he had been when he had first taken office.

'Have I missed Mr. Frederick, sir?'

'By a hair's breadth. Why?'

'This telegram has arrived for him, Mr. Galahad. I thought it might be important.'

'Most unlikely. Probably somebody just wiring him the result of the four o'clock race somewhere. Give it to me, I'll see that he gets it on his return.'

He continued on his way, feeling now rather at a loose end. A sociable man, he wanted someone to talk to. He could of course go and chat with his sister Lady Constance, who was reading a novel on the terrace, but something told him that there would be little profit and entertainment in this. Most of his conversation consisted of anecdotes of his murky past, and Connie was not a good audience for these. He decided on consideration to look up his brother Clarence, with whom it was always a pleasure to exchange ideas, and found that mild and dreamy peer in the library staring fixedly at nothing.

'Ah, there you are, Clarence,' he said, and Lord Emsworth sat up with a startled 'Eh, what?', his stringy body quivering.

'Oh, it's you, Galahad.'

'None other. What's the matter, Clarence?'

'Matter?'

'There's something on your mind. The symptoms are unmistakable. A man whose soul is at rest does not leap like a nymph surprised while bathing when somebody tells him he's there. Confide in me.'

Lord Emsworth was only too glad to do so. A sympathetic listener was precisely what he wanted.

'It's Connie,' he said. 'did you hear what she was saying at breakfast?'

'I didn't come down to breakfast.'

'Ah, then you probably missed it. Well, right in the middle of the meal — I was eating a kippered herring at the time — she told me she was going to get rid of Beach.'

'What! Get rid of *Beach*?'

' "He is so slow," she said. "He wheezes. We ought to have a younger, smarter butler." I was appalled. I choked on my kippered herring.'

'I don't blame you. Blandings without Beach is unthinkable. So is Blandings with what she calls a young, smart butler at the helm. Good God! I can picture the sort of fellows she would get, some acrobatic stripling who would turn somersaults and slide down the banisters. You must put your foot down, Clarence.'

'Who, me?' said Lord Emsworth.

The idea seemed to him too bizarre for consideration. He was, as has been said, a mildly, dreamy man, his sister Constance a forceful and imperious woman modelled on the lines of the late Cleopatra. Nominally he was the master of the house and as such entitled to exercise the Presidential Veto, but in practice Connie's word was always law. Look at the way she made him wear a top hat at the annual village school treat. He had reasoned and pleaded, pointing out in the clearest possible way that for a purely rural festivity of that sort a simple fishing hat would be far more suitable, but every year when August came around there he was, balancing the beastly thing on his head again and just asking the children in the tea tent to throw rock cakes at it.

'I can't put my foot down with Connie.'

'Well, I can, and I'm going to. Fire Beach, indeed! After eighteen years' devoted service. The idea's monstrous.'

'He would of course receive a pension.'

'It's no good her thinking she can gloss it over with any talk about pensions. Wrap it up as she may, the stark fact remains that she's planning to fire him. She must not be allowed to do this frightful thing. Good heavens, you might just as well fire the Archbishop of Canterbury.'

He would have spoken further, but at this moment there came from the stairs outside the slumping of feet, announcing that Freddie was back from the Fanshawes and on his way to his room. Lord Emsworth winced. Like so many aristocratic fathers, he was allergic to younger sons and since going to live in America Freddie had acquired a brisk, go-getter jumpiness which jarred upon him.

'Frederick,' he said with a shudder, and Gally started.

'I've got a telegram for Freddie,' he said. 'I'd better take it up to him.'

'Do,' said Lord Emsworth. 'And I think I will be going and having a look at my flowers.'

He left the room and making for the rose garden pottered slowly to and fro, sniffing at its contents. It was a procedure which as a rule gave him great pleasure, but today his heavy heart found no solace in the scent of roses. Listlessly he returned to the library and took a favourite pig book from its shelf. But even pig books were no palliative. The thought of Beach fading from the Blandings scene, if a man of his bulk could be said to fade, prohibited concentration.

He had sunk into a sombre reverie, when it was interrupted by the entrance of the subject of his gloomy meditations.

'Pardon me, m'lord,' said Beach. 'Mr. Galahad desired me to ask if you would step down to the smoking-room and speak to him.'

'Why can't he come up here?'

'He has sprained his ankle, m'lord. He and Mr. Frederick fell downstairs.'

'Oh?' said Lord Emsworth, not particularly interested. Freddie was always doing odd things. So was Galahad. 'How did that happen?'

'Mr. Galahad informs me that he handed Mr. Frederick a telegram. Mr. Frederick, having opened and perused it, uttered a sharp exclamation, reeled, clutched at Mr. Galahad, and they both fell downstairs. Mr. Frederick, too, has sprained his ankle. He has retired to bed.'

'Bless my soul. Are they in pain?'

'I gather that the agony has to some extent abated. They have been receiving treatment from the kitchen maid. She is a Brownie.'

'She's a *what*?'

'A Brownie, m'lord. I understand it is a species of female Boy Scout. They are instructed in the fundamentals of first aid.'

'Eh? First aid? Oh, you mean first aid,' said Lord Emsworth, reading between the lines. 'Bandages and that sort of thing, what?'

'Precisely, m'lord.'

By the time Lord Emsworth reached the smoking-room the Brownie had completed her ministrations and gone back to her *Screen Gems*. Gally was lying on a sofa, looking not greatly disturbed by his accident. He was smoking a cigar.

'Beach tells me you had a fall,' said Lord Emsworth.

'A stinker,' Gally assented. 'as who wouldn't when an ass of a nephew grabs him at the top of two flights of stairs.'

'Beach seems to think Frederick's action was caused by some bad news in the telegram which you gave to him.'

'That's right. It was from Aggie.'

'Aggie?'

'His wife.'

'I thought her name was Frances.'

'No, Niagara.'

'What a peculiar name.'

'A gush of sentiment on the part of her parents. They spent the honeymoon at Niagara Falls.'

'Ah yes. I have heard of Niagara Falls. People go over them in barrels, do they not? Now there is a thing I would not care to do myself. Most uncomfortable, I should imagine, though no doubt one would get used to it in time. Why was her telegram so disturbing?'

'Because she says she's coming here and will be with us the day after tomorrow.'

'I see no objection to that.'

'Freddie does, and I'll tell you why. He's gone and given her dog to Valerie Fanshawe.'

'Who is Valerie Fanshawe?'

'The daughter of Colonel Fanshawe of Marling Hall, the tally-ho and view-halloo chap. Haven't you met him?'

'No,' said Lord Emsworth, who never met anyone, if he could help it. 'But why should Frances object to Frederick giving this young woman a dog?'

'I didn't say *a* dog. I said *her* dog. Her personal Alsatian, whom she loves to distraction. However, that could be straightened out, I imagine, with a few kisses and a remorseful word or two if Valerie Fanshawe were a girl with a pasty face and spectacles, but unfortunately she isn't. Her hair is golden, her eyes blue, and years of huntin', shootin', and fishin', not to mention swimmin', tennis-playin', and golfin', have rendered her figure lissom and slender. She looks like something out of a beauty chorus, and as you are probably aware the little woman rarely approves of her mate being on chummy terms with someone of that description. Let Aggie get one glimpse of Valerie Fanshawe and learn that Freddie has been showering dogs on her, and she'll probably divorce him.'

'Surely not?'

'It's on the cards. American wives get divorces at the drop of a hat.'

'Bless my soul. What would Frederick do then?'

'Well, her father obviously wouldn't want him working at his dog biscuit emporium. I suppose he would come and live here.'

'What, at the castle?' cried Lord Emsworth, appalled. 'Good God!'

'So you see how serious the situation is. However, I've been giving it intense thought, turning here a stone, exploring there an avenue, and I am glad to say I have found the solution. We must get that dog back before Aggie arrives.'

'You will ask Rosalie Fanshawe to return it?'

'Not quite that. She would never let it go. It will have to be pinched, and that's where you come in.'

'I?'

'Who else is there? Freddie and I are both lying on beds of pain, unable to move, and we can hardly ask Connie to oblige. You are our only mobile force. Your quick intelligence has probably already told you what you have to do. What do people do when they've got a dog. They instruct the butler to let it out for a run last thing at night.'

'Do they?'

'Invariably. Or bang go their carpets. Every dog has its last-thing-at-night outing, and I think we can safely assume that it will be via the back door.'

'What the back door?'

'Via.'

'Oh, via? Yes, yes, quite.'

'So you must pop over to the Fanshawes — say around ten o'clock — and lurk outside their back door till the animal appears, and bring it back here.'

Lord Emsworth stared, aghast.

'But, Galahad!'

'It's no good saying "But, Galahad!" It's got to be done. You don't want Freddie's whole future to turn blue at the edges and go down the drain, do you? Let alone having him at the castle for the rest of his life. Ah, I see you shudder. I thought you

would. And, dash it, it's not much I'm asking of you. Merely to
go and stand in a back garden and scoop in a dog. A child could
do it. If it wasn't that we want to keep the thing a secret just
between ourselves, I'd hand the job over to the Brownie.'

'But what if the dog refused to accompany me? After all,
we've scarcely met.'

'I've thought of that. You must sprinkle your trouser legs
with aniseed. Dogs follow aniseed to the ends of the earth.'

'But I have no aniseed.'

'Beach is bound to be able to lay his hands on some. And
Beach never asks questions. Unlike Connie's young, smart
butler, who would probably be full of them. Oh, Beach,' said
Gally, who had pressed the bell. 'Have we aniseed in the
house?'

'Yes, Mr. Galahad.'

'Bring me a stoup of it, will you?'

'Very good, sir,' said Beach.

If the request surprised him, he did not show it. Your experienced butler never allows himself to look surprised at anything.
He brought the aniseed. At the appointed hour Lord Emsworth
drove off in Freddie's sports model car, smelling to heaven.
And Gally, left alone, lit another cigar and turned his attention
to *The Times* crossword puzzle.

He found it, however, difficult to concentrate on it. This was
not merely because these crossword puzzles had become so abstruse nowadays and he was basically a Sun-god-Ra and Large-
Australian-bird-emu man. Having seen Lord Emsworth off on
his journey, doubts and fears were assailing him. He was wishing he could feel more confident of his brother's chances of
success in the mission which had been entrusted to him. A
lifetime association with him had left him, feeling that the head
of the family was a frail reed on which to lean in an emergency.
His genius for doing the wrong thing was a byword in his circle
of acquaintance.

Which, he was asking himself, of the many ways open to him
for messing everything up would Lord Emsworth select? Drive
the car into a ditch? Go to the wrong house? Or would he forget
all about his assignment and sit by the roadside musing on
pigs? It was impossible to say, and Gally's emotions were similar to those of a General who, having planned a brilliant piece

of strategy, finds himself dubious as to the ability of his troops to carry it out. Generals in such circumstances chew their moustaches in an overwrought sort of way, and Gally would have chewed his, if he had had one.

Heavy breathing sounded outside the door. Beach entered.

'Miss Fanshawe, sir,' he announced.

Gally's acquaintance with Valerie Fanshawe was only a slight one and in the interval since they had last met he had forgotten some of her finer points. Seeing her now, he realised how accurate had been his description of her to Lord Emsworth. In the best and deepest sense of the words she was a dish and a pippin — in short, the very last type of girl to whom a young husband should have given his wife's Alsatian.

'Good evening,' he said. 'You must forgive me for not rising as directed in the books of etiquette. I've sprained my ankle.'

'Oh, I'm sorry,' said Valerie. 'I hope I'm not disturbing you.'

'Not at all.'

'I asked for Mr. Threepwood, forgetting there were two of you. I came to see Freddie.'

'He's gone to bed. He has sprained his ankle.'

The girl seemed puzzled.

'Aren't you getting the cast of characters mixed up?' she said. 'It was you who sprained the ankle.'

'Freddie also.'

'What both of you? What happened?'

'We fell downstairs together.'

'What made you do that?'

'Oh, we thought we would. Can I give Freddie a message?'

'If you wouldn't mind. Tell him that all is well. Did he mention to you that he was trying to sell Father those dog biscuits of his?'

'He did.'

'Well, I approached Father on the subject and he said Oh, all right, he would give him a try. He said he didn't suppose they would actually poison the dumb chums and as I was making such a point of it he'd take a chance.'

'Splendid.'

'And I've brought back the dog.'

It was only the most sensational pieces of news that could

make Gally's monocle drop from his eye. At these words it fell like a shooting star.

'You've done *what*?' he exclaimed, retrieving the monocle and replacing it in order the better to goggle at her.

'He gave me an Alsatian dog this afternoon, and I've brought it back.'

'You mean you don't want it?'

'I want it all right, but I can't have it. The fathead's first act on clocking in was to make a bee line for Father's spaniel and try to assassinate it, the one thing calculated to get himself socially ostracised. Father thinks the world of that spaniel. "Who let this canine paranoiac into the house?" he thundered, foaming at the mouth. I said I had. "Where did you get the foul creature?" he demanded. "Freddie gave him to me," I said. "Then you can damn well take him back to this Freddie, whoever he is" he —'

'Vociferated?'

'Yes, vociferated. "And let me add," he said, "that I am about to get my gun and count ten, and if the animal's still around when I reach that figure, I shall blow his head off at the roots and the Lord have mercy on his soul. Well, I'm pretty quick and I saw right away that what he was hinting at was that he preferred not to associate with the dog, so I've brought him back. I think he went off to the Servants' Hall to have a bite of supper. I shall miss him, of course. Still, easy come, easy go.'

And so saying Valerie Fanshawe, reverting to the subject of Gally's ankle, expressed a hope that he would not have to have it amputated, and withdrew.

If at this moment somebody had started to amputate Gally's ankle, it is hardly probable that he would have noticed it, so centred were his thoughts on this astounding piece of good luck which had befallen a nephew of whom he had always been fond. If, as he supposed, it was the latter's guardian angel who had engineered the happy ending like a conjuror pulling a rabbit out of a hat, he would have liked to slap him on the back and tell him how greatly his efforts were appreciated. Joy cometh in the morning, he told himself, putting the clock forward a little, and by way of celebrating the occasion he rang for Beach and asked him to bring him a whisky and soda.

It was some considerable time before the order was filled, and Beach was full of apologies for his tardiness.

'I must express my regret for being so long, Mr. Galahad. I was detained on the telephone by Colonel Fanshawe.'

'The Fanshawe family seem very much with us tonight. Is there a Mrs. Fanshawe?'

'I understand so, Mr. Galahad.'

'No doubt she will be dropping in shortly. What did the Colonel want?'

'He was asking for his lordship, but I have been unable to locate him.'

'He's gone for a stroll.'

'Indeed? I was not aware. Colonel Fanshawe wished him to come to Marling Hall tomorrow morning in his capacity of Justice of the Peace. It appears that the butler at Marling Hall apprehended a prowler who was lurking in the vicinity of the back door and has locked him in the cellar. Colonel Fanshawe is hoping that his lordship will give him a sharp sentence.'

For the second time that night Gally's monocle had fallen from the parent eye socket. He had not, as we have seen, been sanguine with regard to the possibility of his brother getting through the evening without mishap, but he had not foreseen anything like this. This was outstanding, even for Clarence.

'Beach,' he said, 'this opens up a new line of thought. You speak of a prowler.'

'Yes, sir.'

'Who was lurking at the Fanshawe back door and is now in the Fanshawe cellar.'

'Yes, sir.'

'Well, here's something for your files. The prowler you have in mind was none other than Clarence, ninth Earl of Emsworth.'

'Sir!'

'I assure you. I sent him to Marling Hall on a secret mission, the nature of which I am not empowered to disclose, and how he managed to get copped we shall never know. Suffice it that he did and is now in the cellar. Wine cellar or coal?'

'Coal, I was given to understand, sir.'

'Our task, then, is to get him out of it. Don't speak. I must think, I must think.'

When an ordinary man is trying to formulate a scheme for

extricating his brother from a coal cellar, the procedure is apt to be a lengthy one involving the furrowed brow, the scratched head and the snapped finger, but in the case of a man like Gally this is not so. Only a minimum of time had elapsed before he was able to announce that he had got it.

'Beach!'

'Sir?'

'Go to my bedroom, look in the drawer where the handkerchiefs are, and you will find a small bottle containing white tablets. Bring it to me.'

'Very good, sir.'

'Would this be the bottle to which you refer, sir?' asked Beach, returning a few minutes later.

'That's the one. Now a few necessary facts. Is the butler at the Fanshawes a pal of yours?'

'We are acquainted sir.'

'Then he won't be surprised if you suddenly pay him a call?'

'I imagine not, Mr. Galahad. I sometimes do when I find myself in the neighbourhood of Marling Hall.'

'And on these occasions he sets them up?'

'Sir?'

'You drain a cup or two?'

'Oh yes, sir. I am always offered refreshment.'

'Then it's all over but the cheering. You see this bottle, Beach? It contains what are known as Micky Finns. The name is familiar to you?'

'No, sir.'

'They are a recognised sedative in the United States. When I last went to New York, a great friend of mine, a bartender on Eighth Avenue, happened to speak of them and was shocked to learn that I had none in my possession. They were things, he said which nobody should be without. He gave me a few, assuring me that sooner or later they were bound to come in useful. Hitherto I have had no occasion to make use of them, but I think you will agree that now is the time for them to come to the aid of the party. You follow me, Beach?'

'No, sir.'

'Come, come. You know my methods, apply them. Slip one of these into this butler's drink, and almost immediately you will see him fold up like a tired lily. Your path thus made straight, you proceed to the cellar, unleash his lordship and bring him home.'

'But, Mr. Galahad '

'Now what?'

'I hardly like — '

'Don't stand there making frivolous objections. If Clarence is not extracted from that cellar before tomorrow morning, his name will be mud. He will become a hissing and a byword.'

'Yes, sir, but — '

'And don't overlook another aspect of the matter. Perform this simple task, and there will be no limit to his gratitude. Purses of gold will change hands. Camels bearing apes, ivory and peacocks, all addressed to you, will shortly be calling at the back door of Blandings Castle. You will clean up to an unimaginable extent.'

It was a powerful plea. Beach's two chins, which had been waggling unhappily, ceased to waggle. A light of resolution came into his eyes. He looked like a butler who had stiffened the sinews and summoned up the blood, as recommended by Henry the Fifth.

'Very good, Mr. Galahad,' he said.

Gally resumed his crossword puzzle, more than ever convinced that the compiler of the clues was suffering from softening of the brain, and in due course heavy breathing woke him from the light doze into which he had fallen while endeavouring to read sense into '7 across' and he found that Beach was back from the front. He had the air of one who has recently passed through some great spiritual experience.

'Well?' said Gally. 'All washed up? Everything nice and smooth?'

'Yes, Mr. Galahad.'

'You administered the medium dose for an adult?'

'Yes, Mr. Galahad.'

'And released his lordship?'

'Yes, Mr. Galahad.'

'That's my boy. Where is he?'

'Taking a bath. Mr. Galahad. He was somewhat begrimed. Would there be anything further, sir?'

'Not a thing. You can go to bed and sleep peacefully. Good night.'

'Good night, sir.'

It was some minutes later, while Gally was wrestling with '12 down', that he found his privacy invaded by a caller with whom he had not expected to hobnob. It was very seldom that his sister Constance sought his society. Except for shivering austerely whenever they met, she rarely had much to do with him.

'Oh, hullo, Connie,' he said. 'Are you any good at crossword puzzles?'

Lady Constance did not say 'To hell with crossword puzzles', but it was plain that only her breeding restrained her from doing so. She was in one of those moods of imperious wrath which so often had reduced Lord Emsworth to an apologetic jelly.

'Galahad,' she said. 'Have you seen Beach?'

'Just been chatting with him. Why?'

'I have been ringing for him for half an hour. He really is quite past his duties.'

'Clarence was telling me that that was how you felt about him. He said you were thinking of firing him.'

'I am.'

'I shouldn't.'

'What do you mean?'

'You'll rue the day.'

'I don't understand you.'

'Then let me tell you a little bedtime story.'

'Please do not drivel, Galahad. Really I sometimes think that you have less sense than Clarence.'

'It is a story,' Gally proceeded, ignoring the slur, 'of a feudal devotion to the family interests which it would be hard to overpraise. It shows Beach in so favourable a light that I think you will agree that when you speak of giving him the heave-ho you are talking, if you will forgive me saying so, through the back of your neck.'

'Have you been drinking, Galahad?'

'Only a series of toasts to a butler who will go down in legend and song. Here comes the story.'

He told it well, omitting no detail however slight, and as his narrative unfolded an ashen pallor spread over Lady Constance's face and she began to gulp in a manner which would have interested any doctor specialising in ailments of the thoracic cavity.

'So there you are,' said Gally, concluding. 'Even if you are not touched by his selfless service and lost in admiration of his skill in slipping Micky Finns into people's drinks, you must realise that it would be madness to hand him the pink slip. You can't afford to have him spreading the tale of Clarence's activities all over the county, and you know as well as I do that, if sacked, he will dine out on the thing for months. If I were you, Connie, I would reconsider.'

He eyed the wreck of what had once been a fine upstanding sister with satisfaction. He could read the message of those gulps, and could see that she was reconsidering.

* 3 *

Ukridge Starts a Bank Account

Except that he was quite well-dressed and plainly prosperous, the man a yard or two ahead of me as I walked along Piccadilly looked exactly like my old friend Stanley Featherstonehaugh Ukridge, and I was musing on these odd resemblances and speculating idly as to what my little world would be like if there were two of him in it, when he stopped to peer into a tobacconist's window and I saw that it was Ukridge. It was months since I had seen that battered man of wrath, and though my guardian angel whispered to me that it would mean parting with a loan of five or even ten shillings if I made my presence known, I tapped him on the shoulder.

Usually if you tap Ukridge on the shoulder, he leaps at least six inches into the air, a guilty conscience making him feel that the worst has happened and his sins have found him out, but now he merely beamed, as if being tapped by me had made his day.

'Corky, old horse!' he cried. 'The very man I wanted to see. Come in here while I buy one of those cigarette lighters, and then you must have a bite of lunch with me. And when I say lunch, I don't mean the cup of coffee and roll and butter to which you are accustomed, but something more on the lines of a Babylonian orgy.'

We went into the shop and he paid for the lighter from a wallet stuffed with currency.

'And now,' he said, 'that lunch of which I was speaking. The Ritz is handy.'

It was perhaps tactless of me, but when we had seated ourselves and he had ordered spaciously, I started to prove the mystery of this affluence of his. It occurred to me that he might have gone to live again with his aunt, the wealthy novelist Miss Julia Ukridge, and I asked him if this was so. He said it was not.

'Then where did you get all that money?'

'Honest work, laddie, or anyway I thought it was honest when I took it on. The pay was good. Three pounds a week and no expenses, for of course Percy attended to the household bills. Everything I got was velvet.'

'Who was Percy?'

My employer, and the job with which he entrusted me was selling antique furniture. It came about through my meeting Stout, my aunt's butler, in a pub, and the advice I would give to every young man starting life is Always go into pubs, for you never know whether there won't be someone there who can do you a bit of good. For some minutes after entering the place I had been using all my eloquence and persuasiveness to induce Flossie, the barmaid, to chalk my refreshment up on the slate, my finances at the time being at a rather low ebb. It wasn't easy. I had to extend all my powers. But I won through at last, and I was returning to my seat with a well-filled flagon, when a bloke accosted me and with some surprise I saw it was my Aunt Julia's major domo.

'Hullo,' I said. 'Why aren't you buttling?'

It appeared that he no longer held office. Aunt Julia had given him the sack. This occasioned me no astonishment, for she is a confirmed sacker. You will probably recall that she has bunged me out of the home not once but many times. So I just said 'Tough luck' or something to that effect, and we chatted of this and that. He asked me where I was living now, and I told him, and after a pleasant quarter of an hour we parted, he to go and see his brother, or that's where he said he was going, I to trickle round to the Foreign Office and try to touch George Tupper for a couple of quid, which I was fortunately able to do, he luckily happening to be in amiable mood. Sometimes when you approach Tuppy for a small loan you find him all agitated because mysterious veiled women have been pinching his secret treaties, and on such occasions it is difficult to bend him to your will.

With this addition to my resources I was in a position to pay my landlady the trifling sum I owed her, so when she looked in on me that night as I sat smoking my pipe and wishing I could somehow accumulate a bit of working capital I met her eye without a tremor.

But she had not come to talk finance. She said there was a gentleman downstairs who wanted to see me, and I confess this gave me pause. What with the present worldwide shortage of money affecting us all these days — I had been compelled to let one or two bills run up, and this might well be some creditor whom it would have been embarrassing to meet.

'What sort of man is he?' I asked, and she said he was husky in the voice, which didn't get me much further, and when she added that she had told him I was in, I said she had better send him up, and a few moments later in came a bloke who might have been Stout's brother. Which was as it should have been, for that was what he turned out to be.

'Evening,' he said, and I could see why Mrs. Whatever-her-name-was had described him as husky. His voice was hoarse and muffled. Laryngitis or something, I thought.

'Name of Stout,' he proceeded. 'I think you know my brother Horace.'

'Good lord!' I said. 'Is his name Horace?'

'That's right. And mine's Percy.'

'Are you a butler, too?'

'Silver ring bookie. Or was.'

'You've retired?'

'For a while. Lost my voice calling the odds. And that brings me to what I've come about.'

It was a strange story he had to relate. It seemed that a client of his had let his obligations pile up — a thing I've often wished bookies would let me do — till he owed this Percy a pretty considerable sum, and finally he had settled by handing over a lot of antique furniture. The stuff being no good to Percy, he was anxious to dispose of it if the price was right, and the way to make the price right, he felt, was to enlist the services of someone of persuasive eloquence — someone with the gift of the gab was the way he put it — to sell it for him. Because of course he couldn't do it himself, his bronchial cords having turned blue on him. And his brother Horace, having heard me in action, was convinced that they need seek no further. Any man, Horace said, who could persuade Flossie to give credit for two pints of mild and bitter was the man for Percy. He knew Flossie to be a girl of steel and iron, adamant to the most impassioned pleas, and he said that if he hadn't heard it with his own ears, he wouldn't have believed it possible.

So how about it, Percy asked.

Well, you know me, Corky. First and foremost the level-headed man of business. What, I enquired, was there in it for me, and he said he would give me a commission. I said that I would prefer a salary, and when he suggested five pounds a week with board and lodging thrown in, it was all I could to do to keep from jumping at it, for, as I told you, my financial position was not good. But I managed to sneer loftily, and in the end I got him up to ten.

'You say board and lodging,' I said. 'Where do I board and lodge?'

That, he said, was the most attractive part of the assignment. He wasn't going to take a shop in the metropolis but planned to exhibit his wares in a cottage equipped with honeysuckle, roses and all the fittings down in Kent. One followed his train of thought. Motorists would be passing to and fro in droves and the betting was that at least some of them, seeing the notice on the front gate 'Antique furniture for sale. Genuine period. Guaranteed', would stop off and buy. My Aunt Julia is an aficionada of old furniture and I knew that she had often picked up some good stuff at these wayside emporia. The thing looked to me like a snip, and he said he thought so, too. For mark you, Corky, though you and I wouldn't be seen dead in a ditch with the average antique, there are squads of half-wits who value them highly — showing, I often say, that it takes all sorts to make a world. I told myself that this was going to be good. I slapped him on the back. He slapped me on the back. I shook his hand. He shook my hand. And — what made the whole thing a real love feast — he slipped me an advance of five quid. And the following afternoon found me at Rosemary Cottage in the neighbourhood of Tunbridge Wells, all eagerness to get my nose down to it.

My rosy expectations were fulfilled. For solid comfort there is nothing to beat a jolly bachelor establishment. Women have their merits, of course, but if you are to live the good life, you don't want them around the home. They are always telling you to wipe your boots and they don't like you dining in your shirt sleeves. At Rosemary Cottage we were hampered by none of these restrictions. Liberty Hall about sums it up.

We were a happy little community. Percy had a fund of good stories garnered from his years on the turf, while Horace, though less effervescent as a conversationalist, played the harmonica with considerable skill, a thing I didn't know butlers ever did. The other member of our group was a substantial character named Erb, who was attached to Percy in the capacity of what is called a minder. In case the term is new to you, it meant that if you owed Percy a fiver on the two o'clock at Plumpton and didn't brass up pretty quick, you got Erb on the back of your neck. He was one of those strong silent men who don't speak till they're spoken to, and not often then, but he was fortunately able to play a fair game of Bridge, so we had a four for after supper. Erb was vice-president in charge of the cooking, and I never wish to bite better pork chops than the ones he used to serve up. They melted in the mouth.

Yes, it was an idyllic life, and we lived it to the full. The only thing that cast a shadow was the fact that business might have been brisker. I sold a few of the ghastly objects, but twice I let promising prospects get away from me, and this made me uneasy. I didn't want to get Percy thinking that in entrusting the selling end of the business to me he might have picked the wrong man. With a colossal sum like ten quid a week at stake it behoved me to do some quick thinking, and it wasn't long before I spotted where the trouble lay. My patter lacked the professional note.

You know how it is when you're buying old furniture. You expect the fellow who's selling it to weigh in with a lot of abstruse stuff which doesn't mean a damn thing to you but which you know ought to be there. It's much the same as when you're buying a car. If you aren't handed plenty of applesauce about springs and cam shafts and differential gears and sprockets, you suspect a trap and tell the chap you'll think it over and let him know.

And fortunately I was in a position to correct this flaw in my technique without difficulty. Aunt Julia had shelves of books about old furniture which I could borrow and bone up on, thus acquiring the necessary double-talk, so next morning I set out for The Cedars, Wimbledon Common, full of zeal and the will to win.

I was sorry to be informed by Horace's successor on my arrival that she was in bed with a nasty cold, but he took my name up and came back to say that she could give me five minutes — not longer, because she was expecting the doctor. So I went up and found her sniffing eucalyptus and sneezing a good deal, plainly in rather poor shape. But her sufferings had not impaired her spirit, for the first thing she said to me was that she wouldn't give me a penny, and I was pained to see that that matter of the ormulu clock still rankled. What ormulu clock? Oh, just one which, needing a bit of capital at the time, I pinched from one of the spare rooms, little thinking that its absence would ever be noticed. I hastened to disabuse her of the idea that I had come in the hope of making a touch, and the strain that had threatened to mar the conversation became eased.

'Though I did come to borrow something, Aunt Julia,' I said. 'Do you mind if I take two or three books of yours about antique furniture? I'll return them shortly.'

She sneezed sceptically.

'Or pawn them,' she said. 'Since when have you been interested in antique furniture?'

'I'm selling it.'

'You're *selling* it?' she exclaimed like an echo in the Swiss mountains. 'Do you mean you are working in a shop?'

'Well, not exactly a shop. We conduct our business at a cottage — Rosemary Cottage, to be exact — on the roadside not far from Tunbridge Wells. In this way we catch the motoring trade. The actual selling is in my hands and so far I've done pretty well, but I have not been altogether satisfied with my work. I feel I need more technical stuff, and last night it occurred to me that if I read a few of your books I'd be able to make my sales talk more convincing. So if you will allow me to take a selection from your library — '

She sneezed again, but this time more amiably. She said that if I was really doing some genuine work, she would certainly be delighted to help me, adding in rather poor taste, I thought, that it was about time I stopped messing about and wasting my life as I had been doing. I could have told her, of course, that there is not a moment of the day, except possibly when relaxing over a mild and bitter at the pub, when I am not pondering some vast scheme which will bring me wealth and power, but it didn't seem humane to argue with a woman suffering from a nasty cold.

'Tomorrow, if I am well enough,' she said, 'I will come and see your stock myself.'

'Will you really? That'll be fine.'

'Or perhaps the day after tomorrow. But it's an extraordinary coincidence that you should be selling antique furniture, because — '

'Yes, it was odd that I should have happened to run into Stout.'

'Stout? You mean my butler?'

'Your late butler. He gave me to understand that you had sacked him.'

She sneezed grimly.

'I certainly did. Let me tell you what happened.'

'No, let me tell *you* what happened,' I said, and I related the circumstances of my meeting with Horace, prudently changing the pub to a milk bar. 'I had been having an argument with a fellow at the next table,' I concluded, 'and my eloquence so impressed him that he asked me if I would come down to Rosemary Cottage and sell this antique furniture. He has a brother who recently acquired a lot of it.'

'What!'

~ She sat up in bed, her eyes, though watery, flashing with all the old fire. It was plain that she was about to say something of significance, but before she could speak the door opened and the medicine man appeared, and thinking they were best alone I pushed off and got the books and legged it for the great open spaces.

There was a telephone booth at the end of the road, and I went to it and rang up Percy. These long distance calls run into money, but I felt that he ought to have the good news without delay, no matter what the expense.

It was Horace who answered the phone, and I slipped him the tidings of great joy.

'I've just been seeing my aunt,' I said.

'Oh?' he said.

'She's got a nasty cold,' I said.

'Ah,' he said, and I seemed to detect a note of gratification in his voice, as if he was thinking well of Heaven for having given her a sharp lesson which would teach her to be more careful in future how she went about giving good men the sack.

'But she thinks she'll be all right tomorrow,' I said, 'and the moment the sniffles have ceased and the temperature has returned to normal she's coming down here to inspect our stock. I don't need to tell you what this means. Next to her novels what she loves most in this world is old furniture. It is to her what catnip is to a cat. Confront her with some chair on which nobody could sit with any comfort, and provided it was made by Chippendale, if I've got the name right, the sky's the limit. She's quite likely to buy everything we've got, paying a prince's ransom for each article. I've been with her to sales and with my own eyes have observed her flinging the cash about like a drunken sailor. I know what you're thinking, of course. You feel that after what has passed between you it will be painful for you to meet her again, but you must clench your teeth and stick it like a man. We're all working for the good of the show, so . . . Hullo? Hullo? Are you there?'

He wasn't. He had hung up. Mysterious, I thought, and most disappointing to one who, like myself, had been expecting paeans of joy. However, I was much too bucked to worry about the peculiar behaviour of butlers, and feeling that the occasion called for something in the nature of a celebration I went to the

Foreign Office, gave George Tupper his two quid back and took him out to lunch.

It wasn't a very animated lunch, because Tuppy hardly said a word. He seemed dazed. I've noticed the same thing before in fellows to whom I've repaid a small loan. They get a sort of stunned look, as if they had passed through some great spiritual experience. Odd. But it took more than a silent Tuppy to damp my jocund mood, and I was feeling on top of my form when an hour or two later I crossed the threshold of Rosemary Cottage.

'Yoo-hoo!' I cried. 'I'm back.'

I expected shouts of welcome — not, of course, from Erb, but certainly from Horace and Percy. Instead of which, complete silence reigned. They might all have gone for a walk, but that didn't seem likely, because while Percy sometimes enjoyed a little exercise Horace and Erb hadn't set a foot outdoors since we'd been there. And it was as I stood puzzling over this that I noticed that except for a single table — piecrust tables the things are called — all the furniture had gone, too. I don't mind telling you, Corky, that it baffled me. I could make nothing of it, and I was still making nothing of it when I had that feeling you get sometimes that you are not alone, and, turning, I saw that I had company. Standing beside me was a policeman.

There have been times, I will not conceal it from you, when such a spectacle would have chilled me to the marrow, for you never know what may not ensue, once the Force starts popping up, and it just shows how crystal clear my conscience was that I didn't quail but greeted him with a cheery 'Good evening, officer'.

'Good evening, sir,' he responded courteously. 'Is this Rosemary Cottage?'

'Nothing but. Anything I can do for you?'

'I've come on behalf of Miss Julia Ukridge.'

It seemed strange to me that Aunt Julia should have dealings with the police, but aunts notoriously do the weirdest things, so I received the information with a polite 'Oh really?' adding that she was linked to me by ties of blood, being indeed the sister of my late father, and he said 'Was that so?' and expressed the opinion that it was a small world, a sentiment in which I concurred.

'She was talking of looking me up here,' I said.

S–PP–D

'So I understood, sir. But she was unable to come herself, so she sent her maid with the list. She has a nasty cold.'

'Probably caught it from my aunt.'

'Sir?'

'You said the maid had a nasty cold.'

'No, sir, it's Miss Ukridge who has the nasty cold.'

'Ah, now we have got it straight. What did she send the maid for?'

'To bring us the list of the purloined objects.'

I don't know how it is with you, Corky, but the moment anyone starts talking about purloined objects in my presence I get an uneasy feeling. It was with not a little gooseflesh running down my spine that I gazed at the officer.

'Purloined objects?'

'A number of valuable pieces of furniture. Antiques they call them.'

'Oh, my aunt!'

'Yes, sir, they were her property. They were removed from her residence on Wimbledon Common during her absence. She states that she had gone to Brussels to attend one of these conferences where writers assemble, she being a writer, I understand, and she left her butler in charge of the house. When she came back, the valuable pieces of antique furniture weren't there. The butler, questioned stated that he had taken the afternoon off and gone to the dog races and nobody more surprised than himself when he returned and found the objects had been purloined. He was dismissed, of course, but that didn't help Miss Ukridge's bereavement much. Just locking the stable door after the milk has been spilt, as you might say. And there till this morning the matter rested. But this morning, on information received the lady was led to suspect that the purloined objects were in this Rosemary Cottage, and she got in touch with the local police, who got in touch with us. She thinks, you see, that the butler did it. Worked in with an accomplice, I mean to say, and the two of them got away with the purloined objects, no doubt in a plain van.'

I believe I once asked you, Corky, if during a political discussion in a pub you had ever suddenly been punched on the nose, and if I remember rightly you replied in the negative. But I have been twice — and on each occasion I was conscious of feeling dazed and stunned, like George Tupper when I paid him back the two quid he had lent me and took him to lunch. The illusion that the roof had fallen in and landed on top of my head was extraordinarily vivid. Drinking the constable in with a horrified gaze, I seemed to be looking at two constables, both doing the shimmy.

For his words had removed the scales from my eyes, and I saw Horace and Percy no longer as pleasant business associates but as what they were, a wolf in butler's clothing and a bookie who did not know the difference between right and wrong. Yes, yes, as you say, I have sometimes been compelled by circumstances to pinch an occasional trifle like a clock from my aunt, but there is sharp line drawn between swiping a clock and getting away with a houseful of assorted antique furniture. No doubt they had done it precisely as the constable said, and it must have been absurdly simple. Nothing to it. No, Corky, you are wrong. I do *not* wish I had thought of it myself. I would have scorned such an action, even though knowing the stuff was fully insured and my aunt would be far better off without it.

'The only thing is,' the officer was proceeding. 'I don't see any antique furniture here. There's that table, but it's not on the list. And if there had been antique furniture here, you'd have noticed it. Looks to me as if they'd sent me to the wrong place,' he said, and with a word of regret that I had been troubled he mounted his bicycle and pedalled off.

He left me, as you can readily imagine, with my mind in a turmoil, and you are probably thinking that what was giving me dark circles under the eyes was the discovery that I had been lured by a specious bookie into selling hot furniture and so rendering myself liable to a sharp sentence as an accessory or whatever they call it, but it wasn't. That was bad enough, but what was worse was the realisation that my employer had gone off owing me six weeks' salary. You see, when we had made that gentleman's agreement of ours, he had said that if it was all the same to me, he would prefer to pay me in a lump sum at the end of my term of office instead of week by week, and I had seen no objection. Foolish of me, of course, I cannot impress it on you too strongly, Corky old horse, that if anyone comes offering you money, you should grab it at once and not assent to

any suggestion of payment at some later date. Only so can you
be certain of trousering the stuff.

So, as I say, I stood there draining the bitter cup, and while I
was thus engaged a car stopped in the road outside and a man
came up the garden path.

He was a tall man with grey hair and a funny sort of twist to
his mouth, as if he had just swallowed a bad oyster and was
wishing he hadn't.

'I see you advertise antique furniture,' he said. 'Where do
you keep it?'

I was just about to tell him it had all gone, when he spotted
the piecrust table.

'This looks a nice piece,' he said, and as he spoke I saw in his
eye the unmistakable antique-furniture-collector's gleam which
I had so often seen in my Aunt Julia's at sales, and I quivered
from hair to shoe sole.

You have often commented on my lightning brain and ready
resource, Corky ... well, if it wasn't you, it was somebody else
... and I don't suppose I've ever thought quicker than I did
then. In a sort of blinding flash it came to me that if I could sell
Percy's piecrust table for what he owed me, the thing would be
a stand-off and my position stabilised.

'You bet it's a nice piece,' I said, and proceeded to give him
the works. I was inspired. I doubt if I have ever, not even when
pleading with Flossie that credit was the lifeblood of com-
merce, talked more persuasively. The golden words simply
flowed out, and I could see that I had got him going. It seemed
but a moment before he had produced his chequebook and was
writing me a cheque for sixty pounds.

'Who shall I make it out to?' he asked, and I said S. F.
Ukridge, and he did so and told me where to send the table —
somewhere in the Mayfair district of London — and we parted
on cordial terms.

And not ten minutes after he had driven off, who should
show up but Percy. Yes, Percy in person, the last bloke I had
expected to see. I don't think I described him to you, did I, but
his general appearance was that of a cleanshaven Santa Claus,
and he was looking now more like Santa Claus than ever. Bub-
bling over with good will and joie de vivre. He couldn't have
been chirpier if he had just seen the heavily backed favourite

in the big race stub its toe on a fence and come a purler. 'Hullo, cocky,' he said. 'So you got back.'

Well, you might suppose that after what I had heard from the rozzer I would have started right away to reproach him for his criminal activities and to urge him to give his better self a chance to guide him, but I didn't — partly because it's never any use trying to jerk a bookie's better self to the surface, but principally because I wanted to lose no time in putting our financial affairs on a sound basis. First things first has always been my motto.

'You!' I said. 'I thought you had skipped.'

Have you ever seen a bookie cut to the quick? I hadn't till then. He took it big. There's a word my aunt is fond of using in her novels when the hero has said the wrong thing to the heroine and made her hot under the collar. 'She — ' — what is it? 'Bridled', that's the word I mean. Percy bridled.

'Who me?' he said. 'Without paying you your money? What do you think I am — dishonest?'

I apologised. I said that naturally when I returned and found him gone and all the furniture removed it had started a train of thought.

'Well, I had to get the stuff away before your aunt arrived, didn't I? How much do I owe you? Sixty quid, isn't it? Here you are,' he said, pulling out a wallet the size of an elephant. 'What's that you've got there?'

And I'm blowed if in my emotion at seeing him again I hadn't forgotten all about the twisted lip man's cheque. I endorsed it with a hasty fountain pen and pushed it across. He eyed it with some surprise.

'What's this?'

I may have smirked a bit for I was not a little proud of my recent triumph of salesmanship.

'I just sold the piecrust table to a man who came by in a car.'

'Good boy,' said Percy. 'I knew I hadn't made a mistake in making you vice-president in charge of sales. I've had that table on my hands for months. Took it for a bad debt. How much did you get for it?' He looked at the cheque. 'Sixty quid? Splendid, I only got forty.'

'Eh?'

'From the chap I sold it to this morning.'

'You sold it to somebody this morning?'

'That's right.'

'Then which of them gets it?'

'Why, your chap, of course. He paid more. We've got to do the honest thing.'

'And you'll give your chap his money back?'

'Now don't be silly,' said Percy, and would probably have gone on to reproach me further, but at this moment we had another visitor, a gaunt, lean, spectacled popper-in who looked as if he might be a professor or something on that order.

'I see you advertise antique furniture,' he said. 'I would like to look at . . . Ah,' he said, spotting the table. He nuzzled it a good deal and turned it upside down and once or twice looked as if he were going to smell it.

'Beautiful,' he said. 'A lovely bit of work.'

'You can have it for eighty quid,' said Percy.

The professor smiled one of those gentle smiles.

'I fear it is hardly worth that. When I called it beautiful and lovely, I was alluding to Tancy's workmanship. Ike Tancy, possibly the finest forger of old furniture we have today. At a glance I would say that this was an example of his middle period.'

Percy blew a few bubbles.

'You mean it's a fake! But I was told — '

'Whatever you were told, your informant was mistaken. And may I add that if you persist in this policy of yours of advertising and selling forgeries as genuine antiques, you are liable to come into uncomfortable contact with the Law. It would be wise to remove that notice you have at your gate. Good evening, gentlemen, good evening.'

He left behind him what you might call a strained silence, broken after a moment or so by Percy saying 'Cor!'

'This calls for thought,' he said. 'We've sold that table.'

'Yes.'

'Twice.'

'Yes.'

'And got the money for it.'

'Yes.'

'And it's a fake.'

'Yes.'

'And we passed it off as genuine.'

'Yes.'

'And it seems there's a law against that.'

'Yes.'

'We'd better go to the pub and talk it over.'

'Yes.'

'You be walking on. There's something I want to attend to in the kitchen. By the way, got any matches? I've used all mine.'

I gave him a box and strolled on, deep in thought, and presently he joined me, seeming deep in thought, too. We sat on a stile, both of us plunged in meditation, and then he suddenly uttered an exclamation.

'What a lovely sunset,' he said, 'and how peculiar that the sun's setting in the east. I've never known it to do that before. Why, strike me pink, I believe the cottage is on fire.'

And, Corky, he was perfectly accurate. It was.

Ukridge broke off his narrative, reached for his wallet and laid it on the table preparatory to summoning the waiter to bring the bill. I ventured a question.

'The cottage was reduced to ashes?'

'It was.'

'The piecrust table, too?'

'Yes, I think it must have burned briskly.'

'A bit of luck for you.'

'Very fortunate. Very fortunate.'

'Percy was probably careless with those matches.'

'One feels he must have been. But he certainly brought about the happy ending. Percy's happy. He's made a good thing out of it. I'm happy. I've made a good thing out of it, too. Aunt Julia has the insurance money, so she also is happy, provided of course that her nasty cold has now yielded to treatment. I doubt if the insurance blokes are happy, but we must always remember that the more cash these insurance firms get taken off them, the better it is for them. It makes them more spiritual.'

'How about the two owners of the table?'

'Oh, they've probably forgotten the whole thing by now. Money means nothing to fellows like that. The fellow I sold it to was driving a Rolls-Royce. So looking on the episode from the broad viewpoint . . . I beg your pardon?'

'I said "Good afternoon, Mr. Ukridge" ', said the man who
had suddenly appeared at our table, and I saw Ukridge's jaw
fall like an express lift going down. and I wasn't surprised, for
this was a tall man with grey hair and a curiously twisted
mouth. His eyes, as they bored into Ukridge, were bleak.

'I've been looking for you for a long time and hoping to meet
you again. I'll trouble you for sixty pounds.'

'I haven't got sixty pounds.'

'Spent some of it, eh? Then let's see what you *have* got,' said
the man, turning the contents of the wallet out on the table-
cloth and counting it in an efficient manner. 'Fifty-eight
pounds, six and three pence. That's near enough.'

'But who's going to pay for my lunch?'

'Ah, that we shall never know,' said the man.

But I knew, and it was with a heavy heart that I reached in
my hip pocket for the thin little bundle of pound notes which I
had been hoping would last me for another week.

* 4 *

Success Story

To a man like myself, accustomed to making his mid-day meal
of bread and cheese and a pint of bitter, it was very pleasant to
be sitting in the grill-room of the best restaurant in London,
surrounded by exiled Grand Dukes, chorus girls and the better
type of millionaire, and realising that it wasn't going to cost me
a penny. I beamed at Ukridge, my host, and across the table
with its snowy napery and shining silver he beamed back at me.
He reminded me of a genial old eighteenth-century Squire in
the coloured supplement of a Christmas number presiding over
a dinner to the tenantry.

'Don't spare the caviar, Corky,' he urged cordially.

I said I wouldn't.

'Eat your fill of the whitebait.'

I said I would.

'And when the porterhouse steak comes along, wade into it with your head down and your elbows out at right angles.'

I had already been planning to do this. A man in the dream-like position of sharing lunch at an expensive restaurant with Stanley Featherstonehaugh Ukridge who has announced his intention of paying the score does not stint himself. His impulse is to get his while the conditions prevail. Only when the cigars arrived and the founder of the feast, ignoring the lesser breeds, selected a couple that looked like young torpedoes did I feel impelled to speak a word of warning.

'I suppose you know those cost about ten bob apiece?'

'A bagatelle, laddie. If I find them a cool, fragrant and refreshing smoke, I shall probably order a few boxes.'

I drew at my torpedo in a daze. During the past week or two rumours had been reaching me that S. F. Ukridge, that battered football of Fate, was mysteriously in funds. Men spoke of having met him and having had the half-crowns which they automatically produced waved away with a careless gesture and an amused laugh. But I had not foreseen opulence like this.

'Have you got a job?' I asked. I knew that his aunt, the well-known novelist Miss Julie Ukridge, was always trying to induce him to accept employment, and it seemed to me that she must have secured for him some post which carried with it access to the till.

Ukridge shook his head. 'Better than that, old horse. I have at last succeeded in amassing a bit of working capital, and I am on the eve of making a stupendous fortune. What at, you ask? That, laddie it is too early to say. I shall look about me. But I'll tell you one thing. I shall not become master of ceremonies at an East End boxing joint, which was the walk in life which I was contemplating until quite recently. When did I see you last?'

'Three weeks ago. You touched me for half a crown.'

'Rest assured that you will be repaid a thousandfold. I feed such sums to the birds. Three weeks ago, eh? My story begins about then. It was shortly after that that I met the man in the pub who offered me the position of announcer and master of ceremonies at the Mammoth Palace of Pugilism in Bottleton East.'

'What made him do that?'

'He seemed impressed by my voice. I had just been having a political argument with a deaf Communist at the other end of the bar, and he said he had been looking for a man with a good, carrying voice. He told me that there was an unexpected vacancy, owing to the late incumbent having passed out with cirrhosis of the liver, and said the job was mine, if I cared to take it. Of course, I jumped at it. I had been looking out for something with a future.'

'There was a future in it, you felt?'

'A very bright future. Think it out for yourself. Although the patrons of an institution like that are mostly costermongers and jellied-eel sellers, mingled with these there is a solid body of the intelligentsia of the racing world — trainers, jockeys, stable lads, touts and what not. They all fawn on the master of cere-monies, and it would, I anticipated, be but a question of time before some inside tip was whispered in my ear, enabling me to clean up on an impressive scale. And so I thanked the man profusely and stood him drinks, and it was only after he had about six that he revealed where the catch lay. Quite casually, in the middle of the love feast, he said how much he was look-ing forward to seeing me standing in the ring in my soup-and-fish.'

Ukridge paused dramatically, gazing at me through the pince-nez which he had fastened to his ears, as always, with ginger-beer wire.

'Soup-and-fish, Corky?'

'That upset you?'

'The words were like a slosh on the third waistcoat button.'

'You mean you hadn't got dress clothes?'

'Exactly. Some months previously, when I was living with my aunt, she had bought me a suit, but I had long since sold it to defray living expenses. And the man went on to make it sickeningly clear that a master of ceremonies at the Bottleton East Mammoth Palace of Pugilism simply could not get by without what the French call the *Grande tenue.* One can see, of course, why this is so. An M.C. must impress. He must diffuse a glamour. Costermongers and jellied-eel merchants like to look on him as a being from another and more rarefied world, and faultless evening dress, preferably with a diamond soli-taire in the shirt front, is indispensable.

'So that was that. A stunning blow, you will agree. Many fellows would have fallen crushed beneath it. But not me, Corky. Who was it said: "You can't keep a good man down"?'

'Jonah, taunting the whale.'

'Well, that was what I said to myself. Quickly pulling myself together, I thought the whole thing out, and I saw that all was not lost. A tie, a celluloid collar, a celluloid dickey and a diamond solitaire — you can get them for threepence, if you know where to go — were within my means. The only problem now was securing the actual suit.' He paused, puffing at his cigar.

II

Next day (Ukridge went on) I called upon George Tupper at the Foreign Office, full of the will to win. For the purchase of a secondhand suit of dress clothes it seemed to me that a fiver should be ample, and if you catch old Tuppy in a good mood, on a morning when mysterious veiled women haven't been pinching his draft treaties, you can often work him for a fiver.

But the happy ending was not to be. Tuppy was away on holiday. In my opinion, Corky, these pampered bureaucrats take too many holidays and I don't like it. As one of the people of England, I pay George Tupper his salary, and I expect service.

Still, there it was. I came away and went round to your rooms, only to find that you had locked up all your effects. I wouldn't let this cold, suspicious frame of mind grow upon me, Corky. It's bad for the character.

Well, after that, there was nothing left for me to do but go to The Cedars, Wimbledon Common and, endeavour to get into my aunt's ribs. It was not a task to which I looked forward with a great deal of relish, for we were on distant terms at the time. In fact, when kicking me out of the house, she had firmly stated that she never wished to see my ugly face again.

I did not expect to be effusively welcomed, nor was I. I found her on the point of departure for the Riviera. The car was actually at the door when I arrived, and Oakshott, the butler, was assisting her to enter. On seeing me, she sniffed with a sound like someone tearing a sheet of calico. But she did not actually bat me over the head with her umbrella, so I got in, too, and we drove off.

My first move, of course, was to give her the old oil.

'Well, Aunt Julia,' I began, 'you're looking fine.'

She said I was looking terrible, and asked what I wanted.

'Merely to see you, Aunt Julia. Simply to assure myself that you continue in good health. A nephew's natural anxiety. Still, if you do happen to have a suit of dress clothes on you —'

'Why do you want dress clothes? What has become of the suit I bought you?'

'It is a long and sad story.'

'I suppose you sold it.'

'Certainly not. If you think that of me —'

'I do.'

'In that case, I have nothing more to say.'

'Then you had better get out. Tell Wilson to stop the car.'

I had no intention of telling Wilson to stop the car until I had reasoned and pleaded. I did so all the way to the station, but without avail.

'Ah, well,' I said, at length abandoning the fruitless discussion. We were standing on the platform by that time. 'Then shall we compound for a five, just to keep the books straight?'

Her metallic snort told me that the suggestion had not gone well.

'I would not dream of giving you money. I know you, Stanley. The first thing you would do would be to go and gamble with it.'

And so saying, she got into the train, not even pausing to bestow a farewell kiss, and I stood there shaking in every limb. A boy with a wheeled vehicle tried to interest me in buns, sandwiches and nut chocolate, but I scarcely heard him. Absorbed and distrait, I was examining from every angle the colossal idea which had just leaped into my mind. It was that word 'gamble' that had done it. It is often that way with me. The merest hint is enough.

One of the most interesting phenomena of this modern life of ours, Corky, is the tendency of owners of large houses to convert them for the night, or for as many nights as they can manage without being raided, into gambling joints. They buy half a dozen shemmy shoes, some cards and a few roulette wheels and send out word to the sporting element that the doings are on, and the latter come surging round in shoals. With the customary rake-off for the house the profits are enormous.

Why, then, I was asking myself, should I not, during my aunt's absence, throw The Cedars, Wimbledon Common, open to the pleasure-seeking and scoop in a vast fortune?

I could detect no flaws in the scheme. Always cautious and prudent, I tried hard to find some, but without success.

Once or twice in most lifetimes projects present themselves which the dullest and most naked eye can spot at sight as pure goose, and this was one of them. It was that almost unheard-of rarity, a good thing with no strings attached to it.

Of course, before the venture could become a going concern, there were certain preliminaries that had to be seen to. It would, for instance, be necessary to square Oakshott, who had been left in charge of the premises, and even to cut him in as a partner. For it was he who would have to supply from his savings the capital required for the initial outlay.

Shemmy shoes cost money. So do cards. And you cannot obtain a roulette wheel by mere charm of manner. Obviously, someone would have to do a bit of digging down, and — I, being, as I have shown, a trifle strapped at the moment — everything seemed to point to this butler. But I felt confident that I should be able to make him see that here was his big chance. I had run into him at race meetings once or twice on his afternoon off and knew him to be well equipped with sporting blood. A butler, but one of the boys.

I found Oakshott in his pantry. Dismissing with a gesture the housemaid who was sitting on his knee, I unfolded my proposition. And a few moments later, Corky, you could have knocked me down with a feather! That blighted butler would have none of it. Instead of dancing round in circles on the tips of his toes, strewing roses from his bowler hat and crying 'My benefactor!' he pursed his ruddy lips and dished out an unequivocal refusal to co-operate.

I stared at the man, aghast. Then, thinking that he must have failed to grasp the true inwardness of the thing, with all its infinite promise of money for pickles, I went over it all again, speaking slowly and distinctly. But once more all that sprang to his lips was the raspberry.

'Certainly not, sir,' he said with cold rebuke, staring at me like an archdeacon who has found a choir boy sucking acid drops during divine service. 'Would you have me betray a position of trust?'

I said that that was the idea in a nutshell, and he said I had surprised and shocked him. He then put on his coat, which he had removed in order to cuddle the housemaid, and showed me to the door.

Well, Corky, old horse, you have often seen me totter beneath the buffets of Fate, only to come up smiling again after a brief interval for rest and recuperation. If you were asked to describe me in a word, the adjective you would probably employ is 'resilient', and you would be right. I am resilient.

But on this occasion I am not ashamed to confess that I felt like throwing in the towel and turning my face to the wall, so terrific had been the blow. I wonder if you have ever been slapped in the eye with a wet fish? I was once, during a religious argument with a fishmonger down Bethnal Green way, and the sensation was almost identical.

I had been so confident that I had wealth within my grasp. That was what stunned the soul and numbed the faculties. It had never so much as occurred to me to associate Oakshot with scruples. It was as if I had had in my possession the winning ticket in the Irish Sweep and the promoters had refused to brass up on the ground that they disapproved of lotteries.

III

I left that butler's presence a broken man, and for some days went about in a sort of dream. Then I rallied sufficiently to be able to turn my thoughts, if only languidly, to the practical issues of life. I started to try to make arrangements for floating a loan in connection with the purchase of that suit of dress clothes.

But I was not my old self. Twice, from sheer inertia, I allowed good prospects to duck down side streets and escape untouched. And when one morning I ran across Looney Coote in Piccadilly, and said: 'Hullo, Looney, old man, you're looking fine, can you lend me five?' and he affected to believe that I meant five bob and paid off accordingly. I just trousered the money listlessly. How little it all seemed to matter!

You remember Looney Coote, who was at school with us? As crazy a bimbo as ever went through life one jump ahead of the Lunacy Commissioners, but rich beyond dreams of avarice. If he has lingered in your memory at all, it is probably as the bloke with the loudest laugh and the widest grin of your acquaintance. He should have been certified ten years ago, but nobody can say he isn't sunny.

This morning, however, a cloud was on his brow. He appeared to be brooding on something.

'I'll swear it wasn't straight,' I heard him utter. 'Do you think it could have been straight?'

'What, Looney, old man?' I asked. Five bob isn't much, but one has to be civil.

'This game I've been telling you about.'

He hadn't been telling me about any game, I said and he seemed surprised.

'Haven't I? I thought I had. I've been telling everybody. I went to one of those gambling places last night and got skinned, and, on thinking it over, I'm convinced the game was not on the level.'

The thought of someone as rich as Looney going to gambling places in which I was not financially interested caused the old wound, as you may well imagine, to start throbbing afresh. He asked me what I was snorting about, and I said I wasn't snorting, I was groaning hollowly.

'Where was this? I asked.

'Down Wimbledon way. One of those big houses on the Common.'

Corky, there are times when I have a feeling that I must be clairvoyant. As he spoke these words, I did not merely suspect that he was alluding to the Auntery. I knew.

I clutched his sleeve. 'This house? What was it called?'

'One of those fatheaded names they have out in those parts. The Beeches, or The Weeping Willows, or something.'

'The Cedars?'

'That's right. You know it, do you? Well, I've practically

decided to give that nest of crooks a sharp lesson. I'm going — '

I left him. I wanted to be alone, to think; to ponder, Corky; to turn this ghastly thing over in my mind and examine it in pitiless detail . . . And the more I turned it over and examined it, the more did I recoil in horror from the dark pit into which I was peering. If there is one thing that gives your clean-living, clean-thinking man the pip, it is being compelled to realise to what depths human nature can sink, if it spits on its hands and really gets down to it.

For it was only too revoltingly obvious what had happened. That fiend in butler's shape had done the dirty on me. He stood definitely revealed as a twister of the first order. From the very moment I had started outlining my proposition, he must have resolved to swipe the fruits of my vision and broad outlook. No doubt he had begun putting matters in train directly I left him.

To go and confront him was with me the work of an instant. Well, not exactly an instant, because it's a long way to Wimbledon and a cab was not within my means. This time he was in my aunt's bedroom, having apparently decided to move in there for the duration. I found him reclining in an armchair, smoking a cigar and totting up figures on a sheet of paper, and it was not long before I saw that the fourpence which the journey had cost me was going to be money chucked away.

The idea I had had was that on beholding me the man would quail. But he didn't. I suppose a man like that doesn't quail. Quailing, after all, is the result of conscience doing its stuff, and no doubt his conscience had packed up and handed in its portfolio during his early boyhood. When I towered over him with folded arms and said 'Serpent!' he merely said 'Sir?' and took another suck at the cigar. It made it rather difficult to know what to say next.

However, I got down to it, accusing him roundly of having sneaked my big idea and chiselled me out of my legitimate earnings, and he admitted the charge with a complacent smirk. He even — though with your pure mind, Corky, you will find this hard to believe — thanked me for putting him on to a good thing. Finally, with incredible effrontery, he offered me a fiver in full settlement of all claims, saying that one of these days soft-heartedness would be his ruin.

First, of course, I took a pop at coercing him into a partnership by threatening to inform my aunt, but he waved this away airily by saying that he knew a few things about me too. And that clinched that, because there was a pretty good chance that he did. Then, laddie, I began to speak my mind.

I am a pretty eloquent chap, when stirred, and I can't remember leaving out much. Waving away his degrading bribe, I called him names which I had heard second mates use to ablebodied seamen, and others which the able-bodied seamen had used in describing the second mates later on in the privacy of the foc's'le. Then, turning on my heel, I strode out, pausing at the door to add something which a trimmer had once said to the barman of a Montevideo bar in my presence when the latter had refused to serve him on the ground that he had already had enough. And as I slammed the door, I was filled with a glow of exaltation. It seemed to me that in a difficult situation I had borne myself extremely well.

I don't know, Corky, if you have ever done the fine, dignified thing, refusing to accept money because it was tainted and there wasn't enough of it, but I have always noticed on these occasions that there comes a time when the glow of exaltation begins to ebb. Reason returns to its throne, and you find yourself wondering whether in doing the fine, dignified thing you have not behaved like a silly ass.

With me this happened as I was about halfway through a restorative beer at a pub in Jermyn Street. For it was at that moment that the Bottleton East bloke came in and said he had been looking for me everywhere. What he had to tell me was that I must make my decision about that M.C. job within the next twenty-four hours, as the authorities could not hold it open any longer. And the thought that I had deliberately rejected the fiver which would have placed a secondhand suit of dress clothes within my grasp seemed to gash me like a knife.

I assured him that I would let him know next day without fail, and went out, to pace the streets and ponder.

The whole thing was extraordinarily difficult and complex. On the one hand, pride forbade me to crawl back to that inkysouled butler and tell him that I would accept his grimy money after all. And yet, on the other hand . . .

You see, with old Tuppy out of town I hardly knew where to

turn for the ready, and it was imperative that I obtain employment at an early date. And, apart from that, what the bloke had said about watching me standing in the ring in my soup-and-fish had inflamed my imagination. I could see myself dominating that vast audience with upraised hand and, silence secured, informing it that the next item on the programme would be a four-round bout between Porky Jones of Bermondsey and Slugger Smith of the New Cut, or whoever it might be, and I confess that I found the picture intoxicating. The thought of being the cynosure of all eyes, my lightest word greeted with respectful whistles, moved me proudly. Vanity, of course, but is any of us free from it?

That night I set out once more for The Cedars. I was fully alive to the fact that the pride of the Ukridges was going to get one of the worst wallops it had ever sustained, but there are moments when pride has to take the short end.

IV

It was fortunate that I had gone prepared to have my *amour propre* put through the wringer, for the first thing that happened was that I was refused admittance at the front door because I was not dressed. It was Oakshott himself who inflicted this indignity upon me, bidding me curtly to go round to the back and wait for him in his pantry. He added that he would be glad if I did it quick, as the guests would be arriving shortly. He seemed to think that the sight of what he evidently looked on as a Forgotten Man would distress them.

So I went to the pantry and waited, and presently I could hear cars driving up and merry voices calling to one another and all the other indications of a big night; sounds which, as you may imagine, were like acid to the soul. It must have been nearly an hour before Oakshott condescended to show up, and when he did his manner was curt and forbidding.

'Well?' he said. I tried to think that he had said: 'Well, sir?' but I knew he hadn't. It was only too plain from the very outset that the butler side of him was in complete abeyance. It was more like being granted an audience by a successful company promoter.

I got down to the *res* immediately, informing him — for there is never any sense in wasting time on these occasions — that I had been thinking things over and had decided to take that fiver of his. Whereupon he informed me that he had been thinking it over and had decided not to ruddy well let me have it. There was a nasty glint in his eye, as he spoke, which I didn't like. In the course of a long career I have seen men who wore that indefinable air of not intending to part with fivers, but never one in whom it was so well-marked.

'Your manner this morning was extremely offensive,' he said.

I sank the pride of the Ukridges another notch, and urged him not to allow mere surface manner to influence him. Had he, I asked, never heard of the gruff exterior that covers the heart of gold?

'You called me a —'

'I could not deny it.'

'And a —'

Again I was forced to admit that this was substantially correct.

'And just as you were about to leave you turned at the door and called me a — — —'

I saw that something must be done to check this train of thought.

'Did I hurt your feelings, Oakshott?' I said sympathetically. 'Did I wound you, Oakshott, old pal? It was quite unintentional. If you had been watching my face, you would have seen a twinkle in my eye. I was kidding you, old friend. These pleasantries are not intended to be taken *au pied de la lettre*.'

He said he didn't know what *au pied de la lettre* meant, and I was supplying a rough diagram when an underling of sorts appeared and told him he was wanted at the front. He left me flat, departing without a backward glance, and I started hunting round for the port. There should be some, I felt, in this pantry. 'If butlers come, can port be far behind?' is always a pretty safe rule to go on.

I located it eventually in a cupboard, and took a stimulating swig. It was just what I had been needing. It has frequently happened that a good go in at the port at a critical moment has made all the difference to me as a thinking force. The stuff seems to act directly on the little grey cells, causing them to

flex their muscles and chuck their chests out. A stiff whisky and
soda sometimes has a similar effect, I have noticed, but port
never fails.

It did not fail me now. Quite suddenly, as if I had pressed a
button, there rose before me a picture of my aunt's bedroom,
and in the foreground of it was the mantelpiece with its
handsome clock, worth, I estimated, fully five quid on the
hoof.

My aunt is a woman who likes to surround herself with costly
objects of *vertu*, and who shall blame her? She has the price,
earned with her gifted pen, and if that is how she feels like
spending it, good luck to her, say I. Everywhere throughout her
cultured home you will find rich ornaments, on any one of
which the most cautious pawnbroker would be delighted to
spring a princely sum.

No, Corky, you are wrong. You choose your expressions
carelessly. It was not my intention to *pinch* this clock. The
transaction presented itself to my mind purely in the light of a
temporary loan. No actual figures had been talked by the rep-
resentative of the Bottleton East Mammoth Palace of Pugilism,
but I considered that I was justified in assuming that for such a
post as announcer and master of ceremonies a very substantial
salary might be taken as read. Well, dash it, my predecessor
had died of cirrhosis of the liver. It costs money to die of cirrhosis of the liver. It seemed to me that it would be child's play
to save enough out of that substantial salary in the first week to
de-pop the clock and restore it to its place.

The whole business deal, in short, would be consummated
without my aunt being subjected to any annoyance or incon-
venience whatsoever. It shows what a good whack at the port
will do, when I say that there was actually a moment, as I raced
upstairs, when I told myself that, could she know the facts, she
would be the first to approve and applaud.

I had modified this view somewhat by the time I reached the
door, but I did not allow this to deter me. I flung myself at the
handle and turned it with zip and animation. And you may
picture my chagrin, Corky, when not a damn thing happened.
Oakshott had locked the door and taken away the key, creating
a situation which would have compelled most men to confess

themselves nonplussed, and one which, I must own, rattled even me for a bit.

Then my knowledge of the terrain stood me in good stead. I had spent a considerable amount of time as an inmate of this house — it rarely happens that my aunt kicks me out before the middle of the second week — and I was familiar with its workings. I knew, for instance, that behind the potting shed down by the kitchen garden there was always kept a small but serviceable ladder. I was also aware that my aunt's bedroom had French windows opening on a balcony. With the aid of this ladder and a chisel I would be able to laugh at locksmiths.

Butlers always have chisels, so I went back to the pantry and had no difficulty in finding Oakshott's. There was an electric torch in the same drawer, and I felt that I might need that, too. I had just pocketed these useful objects, when Oakshott came in, and conceive my emotion when I saw that he was carrying a roll the size of a portmanteau. I presumed that he had come to the pantry to bank the stuff. A man in his position, with ready money raining down on him in a steady stream, would naturally wish to cache it from time to time, so as to leave room on his person for more.

The sight of me seemed to give him little or no pleasure. His eyes took on a cold, poached-egg look.

'You still here?'

'Still here,' I assured him.

'It's no good your waiting,' he said churlishly. 'You won't get a smell of that fiver.'

'I need it sorely.'

'So do I.'

'And how easy it would be to give of your plenty. With a wad like that, you'd never know it was gone.'

'It won't be gone.'

I sighed. 'So be it, Oakshott. You won't grudge me a drop of port?'

'You can have some port. I'll have some, too.'

'Shall I hold the money?'

'No.'

'I thought you might want to have your hands free while you

poured. You've been doing well, it would appear. Business is good?'

'Fine. Well, mud in your eye.'

'Skin off your nose,' I replied courteously and we quaffed. He then left me, and I made for the garden.

Passing the drawing-room I could hear sounds of mirth and merriment as the multitude took its pop at the games of chance, putting more cash into Oakshott's pocket as it did so, and I was in two minds about pausing to bung a brick through the window. But this, I saw, though a relief to my feelings, would not further my business interests, so I let it go. I found the ladder and climbed to the balcony, and I was just about to get to work with the chisel when the lights in the room suddenly flashed on, giving me a bit of a jolt.

Speedily recovering, I shoved my nose against the pane and saw Oakshott. He was standing by the chest of drawers, still clutching the roll, and one sensed that, finding me in the pantry, he had decided that this would be a better place to put it. But before he could make his deposit there came a sudden change in the character of the sounds proceeding from below, and he stood listening, rigid like a stag at bay.

My aunt's bedroom, I must mention, is just above the drawing-room, and if there are routs and revels going on in the latter apartment you hears them clearly on the balcony; and inside the room, of course, they come up through the floor. What had arrested Oakshott's attention was the fact that at this juncture there was an abrupt increase in the volume of the noise, together with a feminine scream, or two, followed by a significant silence.

Well, it did not take a man of my experience long to gather what had occurred. I have participated in raids in my time as a patron, as a waiter, as a washer of glasses, and once, in America, actually as a member of the squad conducting the operations, and I know the procedure. What happens is that there is first a universal yell of consternation and the girls all scream, and then all is hushed and everyone stands peering bleakly into the future, trying to think of names and address which will sound reasonably plausible to the gentleman with the note-book.

Briefly, old horse, doom had come upon The Cedars, Wimbledon Common. The joint had been pulled.

V

That Oakshott, also, was able to put two and two together and form a swift diagnosis was shown by the promptness with which he now acted. There was a large wardrobe not far from where he stood, a handsome piece in old walnut, and he dived right into it like a seal going after a chunk of halibut, taking his roll with him.

And I popped in through the French windows and turned the key in the wardrobe door.

Why I did this, I cannot say, except that it seemed a good idea at the time. It was only some moments later that that extraordinary vision for which I have always been so remarkable suggested to me that not only clean fun but solid profit might be derived from the action. Here, it suddenly flashed upon me, was where I might make a bit.

You see, I had studied this Oakshott's psychology, and my researches had left me with the conviction that he was one of those who, finding themselves locked in a wardrobe by a policeman during a raid on premises which they have been employing for illegal purposes, will endeavour to make a dicker with that policeman. On these occasions, as you are probably aware, while the patrons may hope to get off with a fine, mine host himself is in line for the jug, and a butler's liberty is very dear to him. It seemed to me that I was entitled to assume that if Oakshott supposed that matters could be settled out of court, he would not count the cost.

At any rate, the thing seemed a fair sporting venture, so I approached the wardrobe and proceeded to address myself in a crisp, cultured voice — the voice of the younger son of some aristocratic family who, after a year or two at Oxford, has entered the Force *via* the Hendon Police College.

'What,' I enquired, 'are you doing they-ah, Simmons?'

To which I replied, this time using the bass clef and adopting a bit of a Ponder's End accent — for I pictured this Simmons as just some ordinary flatty who had graduated from a board school — 'I've got one of 'em locked in 'ere, sir.'

'Oh, reall-ah?' I said. 'Good work, Simmons. Guard him well. I'm off downstairs.'

I then went to the door, slammed it and paused for a reply.

It did not come immediately, and for a moment I feared that my knowledge of psychology might have let me down. But all was well. I can see now that Oakshott was merely thinking it over and fighting a parsimonious man's battle between his love of liberty and the lust to retain his ill-begotten wealth. Presently there came from within a deprecating, 'Er, officer,' followed by a rustling sound, and there stole out from under the door a fiver.

I gathered it in, and there for a while the matter rested.

I suppose Oakshott realised that when you are buying a policeman's soul you cannot be niggardly, for a few moments later another fiver came stealing out, and I pounced on that, too. After this had gone on for some time, with my current account going up by leaps and bounds, I decided to take my profit and retire from the game. At any minute a systematic search of the premises might be instituted — I couldn't imagine why it hadn't been done already — and if I were to be found on them my presence might be hard to explain. The pure heart and the clean conscience are all very well, but they pay few dividends during a gambling raid, and it seemed to me that I would be better elsewhere. It would not, I felt, be beyond the scope of Oakshott's subtle mind to make the constabulary believe that it was I who had been master of the revels.

So I unlocked the door and nipped out of the window and down the ladder. I have often wondered what Oakshott's reactions were when he stole out and found the place entirely free from P.C. Simmonses.

It was a lovely night, with the stars twinkling away in the firmament, and the garden was very cool and peaceful. I would gladly have lingered and drunk in its fragrance, but I could not but feel that this was not the moment. Many people have complimented me on my nerve of steel, and rightly, but there is a time for reckless courage and a time for prudence. I don't mind admitting that at this particular juncture, with the troops of Midian prowling around, my emotions were those of a cat in a strange alley; and I was anxious to get away from it all.

So marked was this feeling that, as I came abreast of the big water butt outside the kitchen door and heard a noise somewhere in the neighbourhood, as of regulation official boots trampling in the night, I halted with beating heart and raised the lid, intending to get inside. Whereupon, a hand came out and slid a banknote into my grasp. Seeing that my dugout was already occupied, I passed on.

This incident, as you may imagine, made a deep impression on me. It suggested to me that in following the policy of safety first, and concentrating on the swift getaway, I might be passing up something good. If there was gold in the water butt, there might be the same elsewhere. I decided to draw another covert or two before leaving. And to cut a long story short, at the end of ten minutes my balance had substantially increased.

Apparently not all the patrons of The Cedars had been content to remain supinely in the drawing-room when the gendarmerie came popping up through traps. There were those who had acted with that mettle and spirit, which one likes to feel is the birthright of Englishmen, and had hopped out of the window, to distribute themselves here and there about the grounds. One splendid fellow, who came across with a tenner, had snuggled into the cucumber frame. You felt it was the sort of thing Drake or Raleigh would have done.

But now I was naturally anxious to count the takings. A methodical man always likes to know where he stands. It seemed to me that the potting shed was far enough away from the house to be out of the danger zone, so I made for it. And I was crossing the threshold with a gay, if *sotto voce*, song on my lips, when there was a sharp squeal from its dark interior, and I knew that here, too, some poor human waif had found and taken sanctuary.

The next moment the rays of the torch, of which I had quickly pressed the button, revealed the well-known features of my Aunt Julia.

VI

There are times in life, Corky, when the man of iron self-control may be excused for momentarily losing his phlegm. It is a very unnerving thing to find an aunt whom you know to be in the south of France nestling in a potting shed in Wimbledon. A sharp 'Gor-blimey!' escaped my lips, and it was at once evident that the ear of love had recognised the familiar voice.

'Stanley!' she cried.

Usually when my aunt says 'Stanley!' it is a tone of refined exasperation, the ejaculation being preliminary to a thorough ticking-off. But now the general effect was vastly different. Her 'Stanley!' on the present occasion was roughly equivalent to the 'Gawain!' or 'Galahad!' which a distressed damsel in difficulties with a dragon would have uttered on beholding her favourite knight entering the ring with drawn sword.

'Aunt Julia!' I exclaimed. 'What on earth are you doing here?'

In broken accents and in a hushed whisper, starting from time to time at sudden noises, she told her story. It was after all, quite simple. At Cannes, it seemed, she had met a friend, a recent arrival on the Riviera, who knew a man who had told her, the friend, that dark doings were in progress in the old home. And so arresting was this crony's report of the big evenings at The Cedars that my aunt had leaped into the first plane, intent on catching the miscreant responsible on the hop.

'I thought at first it must be you, Stanley.'

I drew myself up with a touch of hauteur. 'Indeed?'

'But my friend said no.'

'I should hope so.'

'She said it was the butler.'

'She was right.'

'And I trusted him implicitly!'

'A pity you did not consult me, Aunt Julia. I could have given you the lowdown on the man's true character.'

'He looks so respectable.'

'Many a man may look respectable, and yet be able to hide at will behind a spiral staircase.'

'You saw through him?'

'Like an X-ray. I suspected that, the moment your back was turned, he would be up to some kind of hell, and I was correct. I came here tonight in the hope of being able to protect your interests.'

'You were gambling?'

I switched on the torch, switching it off again immediately when she asked, with a momentary return to her normal brusque manner, if I wanted to bring every policeman on the premises to the spot.

'If,' I said, 'you were able in that brief instant to get a dekko at my person, Aunt Julia, you will have seen that I am not dressed. At functions like the one at which you have been assisting, the soup-and-fish is obligatory. I possess no soup-and-fish. What happened when you got here?'

'I went into the drawing-room and was just going to order those people out, when a policeman came bursting in and told us that we were all under arrest. I promptly jumped out of the window.'

'Stoutly done, Aunt Julia. The true Ukridge resource.'

'And I took refuge here. What am I to do, Stanley? I must not be found. If I am, how can I convince the police that I am not responsible for the whole thing? The scandal will ruin me. Think, Stanley, think.'

I felt that it would be judicious to rub it in a bit.

'It is an unfortunate state of affairs,' I agreed. 'And while it is not for me to criticise the arrangements which you may see fit to make where your own house is concerned, I cannot but feel that you have brought this on yourself. If you had placed me in charge during your absence ... However, we can go into that later. What I propose to do now is to have a look around to see if the coast is clear. If it is, you will be able to do a quiet sneak over the garden wall. Wait here until I return. If I do not return, you will know that I have fallen a victim to a nephew's devotion.'

Whether or not she said, 'My hero!' I am not certain. It was what she ought to have said, but she is a woman who is apt to miss her cues at times.

However, she did clasp my hand in a fevered clutch, and with a brief word bidding her keep her tail up I went out.

I hadn't gone more than fifty yards when I barged slap into a substantial body. It was coming around a tree, heading east, and I was going around the tree, heading west. We collided like a couple of mastodons mixing it in a primeval swamp. Recovering its balance, it flashed a torch on me and a moment later spoke.

It said: 'Hullo, Ukridge, old top. You here? What a night, what a night, what a night?'

I recognised the voice of Looney Coote. And picture my astonishment, Corky, when, flashing my torch on him, I perceived that he was wearing a policeman's uniform. When I commented on this, he laughed hike a hyena calling to its mate and told me all.

Chagrined at losing his money on the previous night at The Cedars, he had decided to fit himself out at a costumier's and go and raid the place: thus, as he himself put it, giving it the salutary lesson it had been asking for and making it think a bit. Such, Corky, is Looney Coote, and alway has been, I felt, as I had so often felt in my earlier dealings with him, that his spiritual home was definitely Colney Hatch.

Slowly I adjusted my faculties. 'You mean there aren't any cops here?'

'Only me.'

I had to pause at this to master my emotion. When I thought of the intense nervous strain to which I had been subjected and recalled the way I had been tiptoeing about the place and quaking at sudden noises and not letting a twig snap beneath my feet, and all because of this pie-faced half-wit, the temptation to haul off and bust him in the eye was very powerful.

I succeeded in restraining myself, but my manner was cold and severe. 'And the next thing that will happen,' I said, 'is that a bevy of genuine constables will blow in, and you'll get two years hard for impersonating a policeman.'

This rattled him. 'I never thought of that.'

'Muse on it now.'

'The Law gets a bit shirty, does it, if you impersonate policemen?'

'It screams with annoyance.'

'Well, well, well, I'd better leg it, you think?'

'I do.'

'I will. Listen, Ukridge, old man,' said Looney, 'there's something you can do for me. I locked an abundant multitude of the blighters in the drawing-room. I should be vastly obliged if, after I've gone, you would let them out. Here's the key. And, by the way, weren't you saying something this morning about wanting me to lend you money, or something?'

'I was.'

'Would a tenner be enough?'

'I could make it do.'

'Then here you are. Talking of money,' said Looney, 'there

was a strong movement afoot among the blighters to bribe me
to let them go. A good deal of feeling was shown. Amused me, I
must confess. Well, good night, old man. It's been nice seeing
you. Do you think, if I'm stopped by a cop, I could get away
with it by saying I was on my way to a fancy-dress ball?'

'You might try it.'

'I will. Did I give you that tenner?' he said.

'No.'

'Then here you are. Good night, old man, good night.'

I went back to the potting shed and told my aunt that a quick
burst from the garden wall was now in order, and she thanked
me in a trembling voice and kissed me and said she had mis-
judged me. She then popped off at a good speed, and I pushed
along to the drawing-room, forming my plans and schemes
with lightning rapidity as I went. What Looney had said
about the inmates trying to bribe him had stirred me not a
little.

And I am happy to say that he had not deceived me. I found
them most anxious to do business. A few *pourparlers* through
the keyhole and the deal was fixed up at so much per head. The
money was placed in my hands by a stately bird with white
whiskers — He looked as if he might be the President of the
Anti-Gambling League or some equally respectable institution,
and there was no doubt that he had been asking himself quite
often during his vigil what the harvest would be.

There was champagne on the sideboard. When they had all
gone, I sat down and opened a bottle. I felt that I had earned it.

Ukridge paused, and drew luxuriously at his cigar. There
was a look of deep and sublime contentment on his face.

'So there you are, Corky. That is why I am now able to stand
you lunch in this robber's den without a thought for the prices
in the right-hand column. My aunt is all over me, and I am
once more the petted guest in her home. This gives me a base
from which I can operate while making up my mind how best
to employ my enormous capital. For it is enormous. I'd hate to
tell you, old horse, how much I've got. It would be tactless.
You are a struggling young fellow who considers himself lucky
if he snaffles thirty bob for an article in *Interesting Bits*, on
'Famous Lovers of History' or some such rot, and it would be

agony to you to know how rolling I am. You would bite your lip and brood and get all sorts of subversive ideas about the unfair distribution of wealth. It wouldn't be long before we should have you throwing bombs.'

I reassured him. 'Don't worry. I'm not envious. It is enough for me to feel that after this magnificent spread you are going to pay the bill.'

There was a pause. I noticed that behind his gingerbeer-wired pince-nez his eyes had taken on an apologetic look.

'I'm glad you brought that up, Corky,' he said, 'for I was just wondering how to break it to you. I'm extraordinarily sorry, old horse, but I find that I have inadvertently left my money at home. You, I fear, will have to settle up. I'll pay you back next time I see you.'

* 5 *

Bingo Bans the Bomb

As Bingo Little left the offices of *Wee Tots,* the weekly journal which has done so much to mould thought in the nurseries of Great Britain, his brow was furrowed and his heart heavy. The evening was one of those fine evenings which come to London perhaps twice in the course of an English summer, but its beauty struck no answering chord in his soul. The skies were blue, but he was bluer. The sun was smiling, but he could not raise so much as a simper.

When his wife and helpmeet, Rosie M. Banks the popular novelist, had exerted her pull and secured for him the *Wee Tots* editorship, she had said it would be best not to haggle about salary but to take what Henry Cuthbert Purkiss, its proprietor, offered, and he had done so, glad to have even the smallest bit of loose change to rattle in his pocket. But recently there had been unforeseen demands on his purse. Misled by a dream in which he had seen his Aunt Myrtle (relict of the late

J. G. Beenstock) dancing the Twist in a bikini bathing suit out-side Buckingham Palace, he had planked his month's stipend on Merry Widow for the two-thirty at Catterick Bridge, and it had come in fifth in a field of seven. This disaster had left him with a capital of four shillings and threepence, so he had gone to Mr. Purkiss and asked for a raise, and Mr. Purkiss had stared at him incredulously.

'A *what*?' he cried, wincing as if some unfriendly tooth had bitten him in the fleshy part of the leg.

'Just to show your confidence in me and encourage me to rise to new heights of achievement,' said Bingo. 'It would be money well spent,' he pointed out, tenderly picking a piece of fluff off Mr. Purkiss's coat sleeve, for everything helps on these oc-casions.

No business resulted. There were, it seemed, many reasons why Mr. Purkiss found himself unable to accede to the request. He placed these one by one before his right-hand man, and an hour or so later, his daily task completed, the right-hand man went on his way, feeling like a left-hand man.

He told himself that he had not really hoped, for Mr. Purkiss notoriously belonged to — indeed, was the perpetual president of — the slow-with-a-buck school of thought and no one had ever found it easy to induce him to loosen up, but nevertheless the disappointment was substantial. And what put the seal on his depression was that Mrs. Bingo was not available to console him. In normal circumstances he would have hastened to her and cried on her shoulder, but she was unfortunately not among those present. She had gone with Mrs. Purkiss to attend the Founder's Day celebrations at the Brighton seminary where they had been educated and would not be back till tomorrow.

It looked like being a bleak evening. He was in no mood for revelry, but even if he had been, he would have found small scope for it on four shillings and threepence. It seemed to him that his only course was to go to the Drones for a bite of dinner and then return to his lonely home and so to bed, and he was passing through Trafalgar Square en route for Dover Street, where the club was situated, when a sharp exclamation or cry at his side caused him to halt, and looking up he saw that what had interrupted his reverie was a redhaired girl of singular beauty who had that indefinable air of being ready to start something at the drop of a hat which redhaired girls in these disturbed times so often have.

'Oh, hullo,' he said, speaking with the touch of awkwardness customary in young husbands accosted by beautiful girls when their wives are away. He had had no difficulty in recognising her. Her name was Mabel Murgatroyd, and they had met during a police raid on the gambling club they were attending in the days before modern enlightened thought made these resorts legal, and had subsequently spent an agreeable half hour together in a water barrel in somebody's garden. He had not forgotten the incident, and it was plain that it remained green in Miss Murgatroyd's memory also, for she said:

'Well, lord love a duck, if it isn't my old room mate Bingo Little! Fancy meeting you again. How's tricks? Been in any interesting water barrels lately?'

Bingo said No, not lately.

'Nor me. I don't know how it is with you, but I've sort of lost my taste for them. The zest has gone. When you've seen one, I often say, you've seen them all. But there's always something to fill the long hours. I'm going in more for politics these days.'

'What, standing for Parliament?'

'No, banning the bomb and all that.'

'What bomb would that be?'

'The one that's going to blow us all crosseyed unless steps are taken through the proper channels.'

'Ah yes, I know the bomb you mean. No good to man or beast.'

'That's what we feel. When I say "we", I allude to certain of the younger set, of whom I am one. We're protesting against it. Every now and then we march from Aldermaston, protesting like a ton of bricks.'

'Hard on the feet.'

'But very satisfying to the soul. And then we sit a good deal.'

'Sit?'

'That's right.'

'Sit where?'

'Wherever we happen to be. Here, to take an instance at random.'

'What, in the middle of Trafalgar Square? Don't the gendarmerie object?'

'You bet they do. They scoop us up in handfuls.'

'Is that good?'

'Couldn't be better. The papers feature it next morning, and that helps the cause. Ah, here comes a rozzer now, just when we need him. Down with you,' said Mabel Murgatroyd, and seizing Bingo by the wrist she drew him with her to the ground, causing sixteen taxi cabs, three omnibuses and eleven private cars to halt in their tracks, their drivers what-the-helling in no uncertain terms.

It was a moment fraught with discomfort for Bingo. Apart from the fact that all this was doing his trousers no good, he had the feeling that he was making himself conspicuous, a thing he particularly disliked, and in this assumption he was perfectly correct. The suddenness of his descent, too, had made him bite his tongue rather painfully.

But these were, after all, minor inconveniences. What was really disturbing him was the approach of the Government employee to whom his companion had alluded. He was coming alongside at the rate of knots, and his aspect was intimidating to the last degree. His height Bingo estimated at about eight feet seven, and his mood was plainly not sunny.

Nor was this a thing to occasion surprise. For weeks he had been straining the muscles of his back lifting debutantes off London's roadways, and the routine had long since begun to afflict him with ennui. His hearty dislike of debutantes was equalled only by his distaste for their escorts. So now without even saying 'Ho' or 'What's all this?' he attached himself to the persons of Bingo and Miss Murgatroyd and led them from the scene. And in next to no time Bingo found himself in one of Bosher Street's cosy prison cells, due to face the awful majesty of the law on the following morning.

It was not, of course, an entirely novel experience for him. In his bachelor days he had generally found himself in custody on Boat Race night. But he was now a respectable married man and had said goodbye to all that, and it is not too much to say that he burned with shame and remorse. He was also extremely apprehensive. He knew the drill on these occasions. If you wished to escape seven days in the jug, you had to pay a fine of five pounds, and he doubted very much if the M.C. next morning would be satisfied with four shillings and threepence down

and an I O U for the remainder. And what Mrs. Bingo would
have to say when informed on her return that he was in stir, he
did not care to contemplate. She would unquestionably explode
with as loud a report as the bomb which he had been engaged in
banning.

It was consequently with a surge of relief that nearly caused
him to swoon that on facing the magistrate at Bosher Street
Police Court he found him to be one of those likeable magis-
trates who know how to temper justice with mercy. Possibly
because it was his birthday but more probably because he was
influenced by Miss Murgatroyd's radiant beauty, he contented
himself with a mere reprimand, and the erring couple were
allowed to depart without undergoing the extreme penalty of the
law.

Joy, in short, had come in the morning, precisely as the
psalmist said it always did, and it surprised Bingo that his
fellow-lag seemed not to be elated. Her lovely face was pensive,
as if there was something on her mind. In answer to his query as
to why she was not skipping like the high hills she explained
that she was thinking of her white-haired old father, George
Francis Augustus Delamere, fifth Earl of Ippleton, whose
existence at the time when she was making her Trafalgar
Square protest had temporarily slipped her mind.

'When he learns of this, he'll be fit to be tied,' she said.

'But why should he learn of it?'

'He learns of everything. It's a sort of sixth sense. Have you
any loved ones who will have criticisms to make?'

'Only my wife, and she's away.'

'You're in luck,' said Mabel Murgatroyd.

Bingo could not have agreed with her more wholeheartedly.
He and Mrs. Bingo had always conducted their domestic life on
strictly turtle dove lines, but he was a shrewd enough student of
the sex to know that you can push a turtle dove just so far.
Rosie was the sweetest girl in a world where sweet girls are
rather rare, but experience had taught him that, given the right
conditions, she was capable of making her presence felt as perceptibly as one of those hurricanes which becomes so emotional
on reaching Cape Hatteras. It was agreeable to think that there
was no chance of her discovering that in her absence he had

been hobnobbing in the dock at Bosher Street Police Court with red-haired girls of singular beauty.

It was, accordingly with the feeling that if this was not the best of all possible worlds, it would do till another came along that he made his way to the office of *Wee Tots* and lowered his trouser-seat into the editorial chair. He had slept only fitfully on the plank bed with which the authorities had provided him and he had had practically no breakfast, but he felt that the vicissitudes through which he had passed had made him a deeper, graver man, which is always a good thing. With a light heart he addressed himself to the morning's correspondence, collecting material for the Uncle Joe To His Chickabiddies page which was such a popular feature of the paper, and he was reading a communication from Tommy Bootle (aged twelve) about his angora rabbit Kenneth, when the telephone rang and Mrs. Bingo's voice floated over the wire.

'Bingo?'

'Oh, hullo, light of my life. When did you get back?'

'Just now.'

'How did everything go?'

'Quite satisfactorily.'

'Did Ma Purkiss make a speech?'

'Yes, Mrs. Purkiss spoke.'

'Lots of the old college chums there, I suppose?'

'Quite a number.'

'Must have been nice for you meeting them. No doubt you got together and swopped reminiscences of midnight feeds in the dormitory and what the Games Mistress said when she found Maud and Angela smoking cigars behind the gymnasium'

'Quite. Bingo, have you seen the *Mirror* this morning?'

'I have it on my desk, but I haven't looked at it yet.'

'Turn to Page Eight,' said Mrs. Bingo, and there was a click as she rang off.

Bingo did as directed, somewhat puzzled by her anxiety to have him catch up with his reading and also by a certain oddness he had seemed to detect in her voice. Usually it was soft and melodious, easily mistaken for silver bells ringing across a sunlit meadow in Springtime, but in the recent exchanges he thought he had sensed in it a metallic note, and it perplexed him.

But not for long. Scarcely had his eyes rested on the page she had indicated when all was made clear to him and the offices of *Wee Tots* did one of those *entrechats* which Nijinsky used to do in the Russian ballet. It was as if the bomb Miss Murgatroyd disliked so much had been touched off beneath his swivel chair.

Page Eight was mostly pictures. There was one of the Prime Minister opening a bazaar, another of a resident of Chipping Norton, who had just celebrated his hundredth birthday, a third of students rioting in Pernambuco or Mozambique or somewhere. But the one that interested him was the one at the foot of the page. It depicted a large policeman with a girl of singular beauty in one hand and in the other a young man whose features, though somewhat distorted, he was immediately able to recognise. Newspaper photographs tend occasionally to be blurred, but this one was a credit to the artist behind the camera.

It was captioned

THE HON. MABEL MURGATROYD AND FRIENDS

and he sat gazing at it with his eyes protruding in the manner popularised by snails, looking like something stuffed by a taxidermist who had learned his job from a correspondence course and had only got as far as Lesson Three. He had had nasty jars before in his time, for he was one of those unfortunate young men whom Fate seems to enjoy kicking in the seat of the pants, but never one so devastating as this.

Eventually life returned to the rigid limbs, and there swept over him an intense desire for a couple of quick ones. He had got, he realised, to do some very quick thinking and he had long ago learned the lesson that nothing so stimulates the thought processes as a drop of the right stuff. To grab his hat and hasten to the Drones Club was with him the work of an instant. It was not that the stuff was any righter at the Drones than a dozen other resorts that sprang to the mind, but at these ready money had to pass from hand to hand before the pouring started and at the Drones there were no such tedious formalities. You just signed your name.

It occurred to him, moreover, that at the Drones he might find someone who would have something to suggest. And as

luck would have it the first person he ran into in the bar was
Freddie Widgeon, not only one of the finest minds in the club
but a man who all his adult life had been thinking up ingenious
ways of getting himself out of trouble with the other sex.

He related his story, and Freddie, listening sympathetically,
said he had frequently been in the same sort of jam himself.
There was, he said, only one thing to do, and Bingo said that
one would be ample.

'I am assuming,' said Freddie, 'that you haven't the nerve to
come the heavy he-man over the little woman?'

'The what?'

'You know. Looking her in the eye and making her wilt.
Shoving your chin out and saying "Oh, yeah?" and "So
what?" '

Bingo assured him that he was not in error. The suggested
procedure was not within the range of practical politics.

'I thought not,' said Freddie. 'I have seldom been able to
function along those lines myself. It's never easy for the man of
sensibility and refinement. Then what you must do is have an
accident.'

Bingo said he did not grasp the gist, and Freddie explained.

'You know the old gag about women being tough babies in
the ordinary run of things but becoming ministering angels
when pain and anguish wring the brow. There's a lot in it.
Arrange a meeting with Mrs. Bingo in your normal robust state
with not even a cold in the head to help you out, and she will
unquestionably reduce you to a spot of grease. But go to her all
bunged up with splints and bandages, and her heart will melt.
All will be forgiven and forgotten. She will cry "Oh, Bingo
darling!" and weep buckets.'

Bingo passed a thoughtful finger over his chin.

'Splints?'

'That's right.'

'Bandages?'

'Bandages is correct. If possible, bloodstained. The best
thing to do would be to go and get knocked over by a taxi
cab.'

'What's the next best thing?'

'I have sometimes obtained excellent results by falling down
a coal hole and spraining an ankle, but it's not easy to find a

good coal hole these days, so I think you should settle for the taxi.'

'I'm not sure I like the idea of being knocked over by a taxi.'

'You would prefer a lorry?'

'A lorry would be worse.'

'Then I'll tell you what. Go back to the office and drop a typewriter on your foot.'

'But I should break a toe.'

'Exactly. You couldn't do better. Break two or even three. No sense in spoiling the ship for a ha'porth of tar.'

A shudder passed through Bingo.

'I couldn't do it, Freddie old man,' he said, and Freddie clicked his tongue censoriously.

'You're a difficult fellow to help. Then the only thing I can suggest is that you have a double.'

'I've already had one.'

'I don't mean that sort of double. Tell Mrs. Bingo that there must be someone going about the place so like you that the keenest eye is deceived.'

Bingo blossomed like a flower in June. Almost anything that did not involve getting mixed up with taxi cabs and typewriters would have seemed good to him, and this seemed particularly good.

'This business of doubles,' Freddie continued, 'is happening every day. You read books about it. I remember one by Phillips Oppenheim where there was an English bloke who looked just like a German bloke, and the English bloke posed as the German bloke or vice versa, I've forgotten which.'

'And got away with it?'

'With his hair in a braid.'

'Freddie,' said Bingo, 'I believe you've hit it. Gosh, it was a stroke of luck for me running into you.'

But, back at the office, he found his enthusiasm waning. Doubts began to creep in, and what he had supposed to be the scheme of a lifetime lost some of its pristine attractiveness. Mrs. Bingo wrote stories about girls who wanted to be loved for themselves alone and strong silent men who went out into the sunset with stiff upper lips, but she was not without a certain rude intelligence and it was more than possible, he felt, that she might fail to swallow an explanation which he could now see was difficult of ingestion. In its broad general principles Freddie's idea was good, but his story, he could see, would need propping up. It wanted someone to stiffen it with a bit of verisimilitude, and who better for this purpose than Miss Murgatroyd? Her word would be believed. If he could induce her to go to Mrs. Bingo and tell her that she had never set eyes on him in her life and that her Trafalgar Square crony was a cousin of hers of the same name — say — of Ernest Maltravers or Eustace Finch-Finch — he was not fussy about details — the home might yet be saved from the melting pot. He looked up George Francis Augustus Delamere, fifth Earl of Ippleton, in the telephone book and was presently in communication with him.

'Lord Ippleton?'

'Speaking.'

'Good morning.'

'Who says so?'

'My name is Little.'

'And mine,' said the peer, who seemed to be deeply moved, 'is mud.'

'I beg your pardon?'

'Mud.'

'Mud?'

'Yes, mud, after what that ass of a daughter of mine got up to yesterday. I shan't be able to show my face at the club. The boys at the Athenaeum will kid the pants off me. Sitting on her fanny in the middle of Trafalgar Square and getting hauled in by the flatties. I don't know what girls are coming to these days. If my mother had behaved like that, my old governor would have spanked her with the butt end of a slipper, and that's what some responsible person ought to do to young Mabel. "See what you've done, you blighted female," I said to her when she rolled in from the police court. "Blotted the escutcheon, that's what you've done. There hasn't been such a scandal in the family since our ancestress Lady Evangeline forgot to say No to Charles the Second!" I let her have it straight from the shoulder.'

'Girls will be girls,' said Bingo, hoping to soothe.

'Not while I have my health and strength they won't,' said Lord Ippleton.

Bingo saw that nothing was to be gained by pursuing this line of thought. Mabel Murgatroyd's parent was plainly in no mood for abstract discussion of the modern girl. Even at this distance he could hear him gnashing his teeth. Unless it was an electric drill working in the street. He changed the subject.

'I wonder if I could speak to Miss Murgatroyd?'

'Stop wondering.'

'I can't?'

'No.'

'Why not?'

'Because I've shipped her off to her aunt in Edinburgh with strict instructions to stay there till she's got some sense into her fat little head.'

'Oh, gosh!'

'Oh what?'

'Gosh.'

'Why do you say "Gosh"?'

'I couldn't help it.'

'Don't be an ass. Anybody can help saying "Gosh". It only requires will-power. What are you, a reporter?'

'No, just a friend.'

Bingo had never heard the howl of a timber wolf which had stubbed its toe on a rock while hurrying through a Canadian forest, but he thought it must closely resemble the sound that nearly cracked his ear drum.

'A friend, eh? You are, are you? No doubt one of the friends who have led the ivory-skulled little moron astray and started her off on all this escutcheon-blotting. I'd like to skin the lot of you with a blunt knife and dance on your remains. Bounders with beards! You have a beard, of course?'

'No, no beard.'

'Don't try to fool me. All you ghastly outsiders are festooned with the fungus. You flaunt it. Why the devil don't you shave?'

'I shave every day.'

'Is that so? Did you shave today?'

'As a matter of fact, no. I hadn't time. I had rather a busy morning.'

'Then will you do me a personal favour?'

'Certainly, certainly.'

'Go back to whatever germ-ridden den you inhabit and do it

now. And don't use a safety razor, use one of the old-fashioned kind, because then there's a sporting chance that you may sever your carotid artery, which would be what some writer fellow whose name I can't recall described as a consummation devoutly to be wished. Goodbye.'

It was in thoughtful mood that Bingo replaced the receiver. He fancied that he had noticed an animosity in Lord Ippleton's manner — guarded, perhaps, but nevertheless unmistakably animosity — and he was conscious of that feeling of frustration which comes to those who have failed to make friends and influence people. But this was not the main cause of his despondency. What really made the iron enter into his soul was the realisation that with Mabel Murgatroyd in Edinburgh, not to return till the distant date when she had got some sense into her fat little head, he had lost his only chance of putting across that double thing and making it stick. It was, he now saw more clearly than ever, not at all the sort of story a young husband could hope to make convincing without the co-operation of a strong supporting cast. Phillips Oppenheim might have got away with it, but that sort of luck does not happen twice.

It really began to seem as if Freddie Widgeon's typewriter-on-toe sequence was his only resource, and he stood for some time eyeing the substantial machine on which he was wont to turn out wholesome reading matter for the chicks. He even lifted it and held it for a moment poised. But he could not bring himself to let it fall. He hesitated and delayed. If Shakespeare had happened to come by with Ben Jonson, he would have nudged the latter in the ribs and whispered 'See that fellow, rare Ben? He illustrates exactly what I was driving at when I wrote that stuff about letting "I dare not" wait upon "I would" like the poor cat in the adage.'

Finally he gave up the struggle. Replacing the machine, he flung himself into his chair and with his head in his hands uttered a hollow groan. And as he did so, he got the impression that there was a curious echo in the room, but looking up he saw that he had been in error in attributing this to the acoustics. There had been two groans in all, and the second one had proceeded from the lips of H. C. Purkiss. The proprietor of *Wee Tots* was standing in the doorway of his private office, propping himself against the woodwork with an outstretched hand, and it was obvious at a glance that he was not the suave dapper H. C. Purkiss of yesterday. There were dark circles under his eyes, and those eyes could have stepped straight on to any breakfast plate and passed without comment as poached eggs. His nervous system, too, was plainly far from being in midseason form, for when one of the local sparrows, perching on the window sill, uttered a sudden *cheep*, he quivered in every limb and made what looked to Bingo like a spirited attempt to lower the European record for the standing high jump.

'Ah, Mr. Little,' he said huskily. 'Busy at work, I see. Good, good. Is there anything of interest in the morning post bag?'

'Mostly the usual gibbering,' said Bingo. 'Amazing how many of our young subscribers seem to have softening of the brain. There is a letter from Wilfred Waterson (aged seven) about his parrot Percy which would serve him as a passport into any but the most choosy lunatic asylum. He seems to think it miraculous that the bird should invite visitors to have a nut, as if that wasn't the first conversational opening every parrot makes.'

Mr. Purkiss took a more tolerant view.

'I see your point, Mr. Little, but we must not expect old heads on young shoulders. And speaking of heads,' he went on, quivering like an Ouled Nail stomach dancer, 'I wonder if you could oblige me with a couple of aspirins? Or a glass of tomato juice with a drop of Worcester sauce in it would do. You have none? Too bad. It might have brought a certain relief.'

Illumination flashed upon Bingo. If an editor's respect for his proprietor had been less firmly established, it might have flashed sooner.

'Good Lord!' he cried. 'Were you on a toot last night?'

Mr. Purkiss waved a deprecating hand, nearly overbalancing in the process.

'Toot is a harsh word, Mr. Little. I confess that in Mrs. Purkiss's absence I attempted to alleviate my loneliness by joining a group of friends who wished to play poker. It was a lengthy session, concluding only an hour ago, and it is possible that in the course of the evening I may have exceeded — slightly — my customary intake of alcholic refreshment. It seemed to be expected of me, and I did not like to refuse. But when you use the word "toot" . . .'

Bingo had no wish to be severe, but except when throwing together stories to tell Mrs. Bingo he liked accuracy.

'It sounds like a toot to me,' he said. 'The facts all go to show that . . .'

He broke off. An idea of amazing brilliance had struck him. Twenty-four hours ago he would never have had the moral courage to suggest such a thing, but now that H. C. Purkiss had shown himself to be one of the boys — poker parties in the home and all that — he was convinced that if he, Bingo, begged him, Purkiss, to say that he, Bingo, had been with him, Purkiss, last night, he, Purkiss, would not have the inhumanity to deny him, Bingo, a little favour which would cost him, Purkiss, nothing and would put him, Bingo, on velvet. For Mrs. Bingo would not dream of disbelieving a statement from such a source. And he had just opened his lips to speak, when Mr. Purkiss resumed his remarks.

'Perhaps you are right, Mr. Little. Quite possible toot may be the *mot juste.* But however we describe the episode, one thing is certain, it has placed me in a position of the gravest peril. The party — "party" is surely a nicer word — took place at the house of one of the friends I was mentioning, and I am informed by my maidservant that Mrs. Purkiss made no fewer than five attempts to reach me on the telephone last night — at 10.30 p.m., at 11.15 p.m., shortly after midnight, at 2 a.m., and again at 4.20 a.m., and I greatly fear . . .'

'You mean you were away from home all *night*?'

'Alas, Mr. Little, I was.'

Bingo's heart sank. He would have reeled beneath the shock, had he not been seated. This was the end. This put the frosting on the cake. Impossible now to assure Mrs. Bingo that he had been with Mr. Purkiss during the hours he had spent in his Bosher Street cell. So poignant was his anguish that he uttered a piercing cry, and Mr. Purkiss rose into the air, dislodging some plaster from the ceiling with the top of his head.

'So,' the stricken man went on, having returned to terra firma, 'I should be infinitely grateful to you, Mr. Little, if you would vouch for it that I was with you till an advanced hour at your home. It would, indeed, do no harm if you were to tell Mrs. Purkiss that we sat up so long discussing matters of office policy that you allowed me to spend the night in your spare room.'

Bingo drew a deep breath. It has been sufficiently established that the proprietor of *Wee Tots* was not as of even date easy on the eye, but to him he seemed a lovely spectacle. He could not have gazed on him with more appreciation if he had been the Taj Mahal by moonlight.

His manner, however, was austere. A voice had seemed to whisper in his ear that this was where, if he played his cards right, he could do himself a bit of good. There was, so he had learned from a reliable source, a tide in the affairs of men which, taken at the flood, leads on to fortune.

He frowned, at the same time pursing his lips.

'Am I to understand, Purkiss, that you are asking me to tell a deliberate falsehood?'

'You would be doing me a great kindness.'

In order to speak, Bingo had been obliged to unpurse his lips, but he still frowned.

'I'm not sure,' he said coldly, 'that I feel like doing you kindnesses. Yesterday I asked you for a raise of salary and you curtly refused.'

'Not curtly. Surely not curtly, Mr. Little.'

'Well, fairly curtly.'

'Yes, I remember. But I have given the matter thought, and I am now prepared to increase your stipend by — shall we say ten pounds a month?'

'Make it fifty.'

'Fifty!'

'Well, call it forty.'

'You would not consider thirty?'

'Certainly not.'

'Very well.'

'You agree?'

'I do.'

The telephone rang.

'Ah,' said Bingo. 'That is probably my wife again. Hullo?'

'Bingo?'

'Oh, hullo, moon of my delight. What became of you when we were talking before? Why did you buzz off like a jack rabbit?'

'I had to go and look after Mrs. Purkiss.'

'Something wrong with her?'

'She was distracted because Mr. Purkiss was not at home all night.'

Bingo laughed a jolly laugh.

'Of course he wasn't. He was with me.'

'What!'

'Certainly. We had office matters to discuss, and I took him home with me. We sat up so long that I put him up in the spare room. He spent the night there.'

There was a long silence at the other end of the wire. Then Mrs. Bingo spoke.

'But that photograph!'

'Which photograph? Oh, you mean the one in the paper, and I think I know what's in your mind. It looked rather like me, didn't it? I was quite surprised. I've often heard of this thing of fellows having doubles, but I've never come across an instance of it before. Except in books, of course. I remember one by Phillips Oppenheim where there was an English bloke who looked just like a German bloke, and the English bloke posed with complete success as the German bloke or vice versa I've forgotten which. I believe it caused quite a bit of confusion. But, getting back to that photograph, obviously if I spent the night with Mr. Purkiss I couldn't have spent it in a dungeon cell, as my double presumably did. But perhaps you would care to have a word with Mr. Purkiss, who is here at my side. For you, Purkiss,' said Bingo, handing him the telephone.

* 6 *

Stylish Stouts

'Ah, there you are, Mr. Little,' said H. C. Purkiss. 'Are you engaged for dinner tonight?'

Bingo replied . . .

But before recording Bingo's reply it is necessary to go back a step or two and do what is known to lawyers as laying the proper foundation.

It was the practice of H. C. Purkiss, proprietor of *Wee Tots*, the journal for the nursery and the home, to take his annual holiday in July. This meant that Bingo, the paper's up-and-coming young editor, had to take his in June or August. This year, as in the previous year, he had done so towards the middle of the former month, and he rejoined the human herd, looking bronzed and fit, a few days before the Eton and Harrow match. And he was strolling along Piccadilly, thinking of this and that, when he ran into his fellow clubman Catsmeat Potter-Pirbright (Claude Cattermole, the popular actor of juvenile roles) and after a conversation of great brilliance but too long to be given in detail Catsmeat asked him if he would care to have a couple of seats next week for the dramatic entertainment in which he was appearing. And Bingo, enchanted at the prospect of getting into a theatre on the nod, jumped at the offer like a rising trout. He looked forward with bright enthusiasm to seeing Catsmeat bound on with a racquet at the beginning of act one shouting 'Tennis, anyone?' as he presumed he would do.

There remained the problem of choosing a partner for the round of pleasure. His wife, Rosie M. Banks the widely read author of novels of sentiment, was at Droitwich with her mother and Algernon Aubrey, the bouncing baby who had recently appeared on the London scene. He thought of Mr. Purkiss, but rejected the idea. Eventually he decided to go and ask his Aunt Myrtle, Mrs. J. G. Beenstock, if she would like to come along. It would mean an uncomfortable evening. She would overflow into his seat, for she was as stout a woman as ever paled at the sight of a diet sheet and, had she been in Parliament, would have counted two on a division, but she was a lonely, or fairly lonely, widow and he felt it would be a kindly act to bring a little sunshine into her life. He ankled round, accordingly, to her house and his ring at the bell was answered by Wilberforce, who regretted to say that Madam was not in residence, being on one of those Mediterranean cruises. He was anticipating her return, said Wilberforce, either tomorrow or the day after, and Bingo was about to push off when the butler, putting a hand over his mouth and speaking from the side of it, said in a hushed whisper:

'Do you want to make a packet, Mr. Richard?'

A packet being what above all things Bingo was always desirous of making, his reply in the affirmative was both immediate and eager.

'Put your shirt on Whistler's Mother for the two o'clock at Hurst Park tomorrow,' whispered Wilberforce, and having added that prompt action would enable him to get odds of eight to one he went about his butlerine duties, leaving Bingo in a frame of mind which someone like the late Gustave Flaubert, who was fussy about the right word, would have described as chaotic.

What to do, what to do, he was asking himself, this way and that dividing the swift mind. On the one hand, Wilberforce was a knowledgeable man who enjoyed a wide acquaintance with jockeys, race course touts, stable cats and others who knew a bit. His judgment of form could surely be trusted. On the other hand, Mrs. Bingo, who like so many wives was deficient in sporting blood, had specifically forbidden him to wager on racehorses and he shrank from the scene which must inevitably ensue, should the good thing come unstuck and she found out about it. The situation was unquestionably one that provided food for thought.

And then he realised that his problem was after all only an academic one, for he was down to his last five bob with nothing coming in till pay day, and with bookies, money has to change hands before a deal can be consummated. If a dozen Whistler's Mothers were entered for a dozen two o'clock races, he was in no position to do anything about it.

It was quite a relief really to have the thing settled for him, and he was in excellent spirits when he got home. He took off his shoes, mixed himself a mild gin and tonic, and was about to curl up on the sofa with a good book, when the telephone rang.

A well-remembered voice came over the wire.

'Sweetie?'

'Oh, hullo, sweetie.'

'When did you get back?'

'Just clocked in.'

'How are you?'

'I'm fine, though missing you sorely. And you?'

'I'm fine.'

'And Algy?'

'He's fine.'

'And your mother?'

'Only pretty good. She swallowed some water at the brine baths this morning. She's better now, but she still makes a funny whistling sound when she breathes.'

The receiver shook in Bingo's right hand. The good book with which he had been about to curl up fell limply from his left. He had always been a great believer in signs and omens, and if this wasn't a sign and omen he didn't know a sign and omen when he saw one.

'Did you say your mother was a Whistler's — or rather a whistling mother?' he gasped at length.

'Yes, it sounds just like gas escaping from a pipe.'

Bingo tottered to a chair, taking the telephone with him. He was feeling bitter, and he had every excuse for feeling bitter. Here he was with a sure thing at his disposal, barred from cashing in on it for lack of funds. Affluence had been offered to him on a plate with watercress round it, and he must let it go because he did not possess the necessary entrance fee. He could not have had a more vivid appreciation of the irony of life if he had been Thomas Hardy.

'Oh, by the way,' said Mrs. Bingo, 'what I really rang up about. You know it's Algy's birthday next week. I've bought him a rattle and some sort of woolly animal, but I think we ought to put something in his little wee bank account, as we did last year. So I'm sending you ten pounds. Goodbye, sweetie, I must rush I'm having a perm and I'm late already.'

She rang off, and Bingo sat tingling in every limb. He continued to tingle not only till bedtime but later. Far into the silent night he tossed on his pillow, a prey to the hopes and fears he had experienced when Wilberforce had mooted the idea of his making a packet. Once more the question 'What to do?' raced through his fevered mind. It was not qualms about touching his offspring for a temporary loan that made him waver and hesitate. That end of it was all right. Any son of his, he knew, would be only too glad to finance a father's sporting venture, particularly when that sporting venture was in the deepest and fullest sense of the words money for jam. And he did not need to tell the child that when the bookie brassed up on settling day he would get his cut and find his wee bank account augmented not by one tenner but by two.

No, it was the thought of Mrs. Bingo that made him irresolute. Wilberforce was confident that Whistler's Mother would defy all competition, giving the impression that having a bit on her was virtually tantamount to finding money in the street, but these good things sometimes go wrong. The poet Burns has pointed this out to his public. 'Gang agley' was how he put it, for he did not spell very well, but it meant the same thing. And if this one went agley, what would the harvest be? He fell asleep still wondering if he dared risk it.

But the next morning he was his courageous self again. The luncheon hour found him in the offices of Charles ('Charlie Always Pays') Pikelet, the well-known turf accountant, handing over the cash, and at 2.13 sharp he was in a chair in the

Drones Club smoking-room with his face buried in his hands. The result of the two o'clock race at Hurst Park had just come over the tape, and the following horses had reached journey's end ahead of Whistler's Mother — Harbour Lights, Sweet Pea, Scotch Mist, Parson's Pleasure, Brian Boru, Ariadne and Christopher Columbus. Eight ran. Unlike Wilberforce, the poet Burns had known what he was talking about.

How long he sat there, a broken man, he could not have said. When he did emerge from his coma, it was to become aware that a good deal of activity was in progress in the smoking-room. A Crumpet was sitting at a table near the door with a pencil in his hand and a sheet of paper before him, and there was a constant flowing of members to this table. He could make nothing of it, and he turned for an explanation to Catsmeat Potter-Pirbright, who had just taken the chair next to him.

'What's going on?' he asked.

'It was the Fat Uncles Sweep,' Catsmeat said.

'The what?'

Catsmeat was amazed.

'Do you mean to say you don't know about the Fat Uncles Sweep? Weren't you here last year when it started?'

'I must have been away.'

'The race is run on the first day of the Eton and Harrow match.'

'Ah, then I was away. I always have to take my holiday early, and don't get back for the Eton and Harrow match. I did this time, but not as a rule. What is it?'

Catsmeat explained. An intelligent Drone, he said, himself the possessor of one of the fattest uncles in London, had noticed how many of his fellow members had fat uncles, too, and had felt it a waste of good material not to make these the basis of a sporting contest similar, though on a smaller scale, to those in operation in Ireland and Calcutta. The mechanics of the thing were simple. You entered your uncle, others entered theirs, the names were shaken up in a hat and the judging was done by McGarry, the club bartender, who had the uncanny gift of being able to estimate to an ounce the weight of anything from a Pekinese to a Covent Garden soprano, just looking at it.

'And the fellow who draws the winning ticket,' Catsmeat concluded, 'scoops the jackpot. Except, of course, for the fifty pounds allocated to the winning uncle's owner as prize money.'

A loud gasp escaped Bingo. A passer-by would have noticed that his eyes were shining with a strange light.

'Fifty pounds?'

'That's right.'

Bingo shot from his chair and gazed wildly about the room.

'Where's Oofy?' he cried, alluding to Oofy Prosser, the club's millionaire.

'In the bar, I believe. What do you want him for?'

'I want to enter my Aunt Myrtle and sell him a piece of her to enable me to meet current expenses.'

'But —'

'Don't sit there saying "But". When's the drawing?'

'Three days from now.'

'Plenty of time. I'll approach him at once.'

'But —'

'That word again! What's bothering you? If you think Oofy won't make a deal, you're wrong. He's a business man. He'll know he'll be on a sure thing. You've seen my Aunt Myrtle and you can testify to her stoutness. There can't possibly be an uncle fatter than her. Let's go and find Oofy now and have him draw up an agreement.'

'But aunts aren't eligible. Only uncles.'

Bingo stared at him, aghast.

'What ... what did you say?'

Catsmeat repeated his statement, and Bingo quivered in every limb.

'You mean to tell me that if a man has the stoutest aunt in the West End of London, an aunt who, if she were not independently wealthy, could be making a good living as the Fat Woman in a circus, he can't cash in on her?'

'I'm afraid not.'

'What a monstrous thing! Are you sure?'

'Quite sure. It's all in the book of rules.'

It was a Bingo with heart bowed down and feeling more like a toad beneath a harrow than the editor of a journal for the nursery and the home who returned to the offices of *Wee Tots* and endeavoured to concentrate on the letters which had come in from subscribers for the Correspondence page. He took up a communication from Edwin Waters (aged seven) about his Siamese cat Miggles, but he found his attention wandering. He found the same difficulty in becoming engrossed in four pages from Alexander Allbright (aged six) about his tortoise Shelley, and he had started on a lengthy screed from Anita Ellsworth (aged eight) which seemed to have to do with a canary of the name of Birdie, when the door of the inner office opened and Mr. Purkiss appeared.

'Ah, there you are, Mr. Little,' said H. C. Purkiss. 'Are you engaged for dinner tonight?'

Which, if you remember, is where we came in.

Bingo replied hollowly that he was not, and might have added that if his employer was about to invite him to share the evening meal, he was prepared to defend himself with tooth and claw.

'I thought that Mrs. Little might be having guests.'

'She's at Droitwich with her mother. Her mother is taking the brine baths. She has rheumatism.'

'Splendid. Excellent. Capital,' said Mr. Purkiss, hastening to explain that it was not the fact of Bingo's mother-in-law having trouble with her joints that exhilarated him. 'Then you are free, I am delighted to hear it. Tell me, Mr. Little, are you familiar with the work of an American author of juvenile fiction named Kirk Rockaway? No? I am not surprised. He is almost unknown on this side of the Atlantic, but his Peter the Pup, Kootchy the Kitten and Hilda the Hen are, I understand, required reading for the children of his native country. I have glanced at some of his works and they are superb. He is just the circulation-builder *Wee Tots* needs. He is here in London on a visit.'

Bingo was a conscientious editor. His personal affairs might be in a state of extreme disorder, but he was always able to shelve his private worries when it was a matter of doing his paper a bit of good.

'We'd better go after him before those blighters at *Small Fry* get ahead of us,' he said.

Mr. Purkiss smiled triumphantly.

'I have already done so. I met him at a tea party given in his honour yesterday, and he has accepted an invitation to dine with me tonight at Barribault's Hotel.'

'That's good.'

'And this,' said Mr. Purkiss, 'is better. At that tea party a most significant thing happened. Somebody mentioned Mrs. Little's books, and he turned out to be a warm admirer of them. He spoke of them with unbounded enthusiasm. You see what I am about to say, Mr. Little?'

'He wants her autograph?'

'That, of course, and I assured him that he could rely on her. But obviously tonight's arrangements must be changed. You, not I, must be his host. As Mrs. Little's husband, you are the one he will want to meet. I will ring him up now.'

Mr. Purkiss went back to his room, to return a few moments later, beaming.

'All is settled, Mr. Little. I had, I am afraid, to stoop to a slight prevarication. I told him I was subject to a bronchial affection which rendered it inadvisable for me to venture out at night, but that my editor, the husband of Rosie M. Banks, would be there in my place. He was all enthusiasm and is looking forward keenly to meeting you. I will, of course, defray your expenses. Here are ten pounds. That will amply cover the cost of dinner, for Mr. Rockaway tells me he is a lifelong tee-totaller, so there will be no wine bill. You can bring me the change tomorrow.'

To say that Bingo was elated at the prospect of an evening out with a man who wrote about hens and kittens and drank only lemonade would be incorrect. Nor did he fail to writhe at the thought that Life had sprung another of its ironies on him by putting ten pounds in his trouser pocket but making it impossible for him to divert the sum into Algernon Aubrey's little wee bank account. For one mad moment he toyed with the idea of not giving Kirk Rockaway dinner and holding on to Mr. Purkiss's tenner, but he discarded it. If he stood Kirk Rockaway up, the hen and kitten specialist would be bound to contact Mr. Purkiss and ask him what the hell, and Mr. Purkiss, informed of the circumstances, would instantly relieve his young assistant of his editorial chair, Mrs. Bingo would want to know why, and . . . but here Bingo preferred to abandon this train of thought. Shortly before eight o'clock he was in the lobby of Barribault's Hotel, and in due course Kirk Rockaway appeared.

One says 'appeared', but the word would not have satisfied Gustave Flaubert. He would have suggested some such alternative as 'loomed up' or 'came waddling along' as being more exact, for the author of *Kootchy the Kitten* and *Peter the Pup* was one of the fattest men that ever broke a try-your-weight machine. He looked as if he had been eating nothing but starchy foods since early boyhood, and it saddened Bingo to think of all this wonderful material going to waste. If only this man could have been his uncle, he felt wistfully. Oofy Prosser would have paid twenty pounds for a mere third of him.

'Mr. Little?' said this human hippopotamus. He grasped Bingo's hand and subjected him to a pop-eyed but reverent gaze. 'Well, well, well!' he said. 'This is certainly a great moment for me. Mrs. Little's books have been an inspiration to me for years. I read them incessantly and I am not ashamed to say with tears in my eyes. She seems to make the world a better, sweeter place. I am looking forward to having the privilege of meeting her. How is she? Well, I hope?'

'Oh, fine.'

'That's good,' said Kirk Rockaway, and then he uttered these astounding words:

'Let's get one thing straight, Mr. Little. The money of Rosie M. Banks's husband is no good in this hotel. Dismiss all thoughts of picking up the tab tonight. This dinner is on me.'

'What!'

'Yes sir. I wouldn't be able to look Mrs. Little in the face if I let you pay for it.'

The lobby of Barribault's Hotel is solidly constructed and the last thing in the world to break suddenly into the old fashioned buck-and-wing dance, but to Bingo it seemed that it was forgetting itself in this manner. There were two pillars in its centre, and he distinctly saw them do a kick upwards and another kick sideways. Ecstasy for a moment kept him dumb. Then he was able to murmur that this was awfully kind of Mr. Rockaway.

'Don't give it a thought,' said Kirk Rockaway. 'Let's go in, shall we?'

Over the smoked salmon what conversation took place was confined to Bingo's host. Bingo himself still felt incapable of speech. The realisation that by this miracle at the eleventh hour he had been saved from the fate that is worse than death — viz having to confess the awful truth to Mrs. Bingo and listen to her comments on his recent activities, seemed to have paralysed his vocal cords. He was still dazed and silent when the soup arrived.

The evening was warm and it had been quite a walk through the lobby and into the restaurant and across the restaurant to their table, and Kirk Rockaway, evidently unused to exercise, had felt the strain. By the time the soup came, beads of perspiration had begun to form on his forehead, and after about the fifth spoonful he reached in his breast pocket for a handkerchief. He pulled it out and with it came a cabinet size photograph which shot through the air and fell into Bingo's plate. And as Bingo fished it from the purée and started to dry it with his napkin, something familiar about it struck his attention. It portrayed a woman of ample dimensions looking over her shoulder in an arch sort of way, and with a good deal of surprise he recognised her as Mrs. J. G. Beenstock, the last person he would have expected to find in his soup.

'Well, well,' he said. 'So you know my aunt?'

'Your what?'

'My aunt.'

Kirk Rockaway stared at him, astounded.

'Is that divine woman your aunt?'

'That's just what she is.'

'You amaze me!'

'I'm amazed too. What are you doing going about with her photograph next to your heart?'

Kirk Rockaway hesitated for a moment. He seemed to be blushing, though it was hard to say for certain, his face from the start having been tomatoesque. Finally he spoke.

'Shall I tell you something?' he said.

'Do.'

'I've come all the way from Oakland, San Francisco, to marry her.'

It was Bingo's turn to stare, astounded.

'You mean you and Aunt Myrtle are engaged?'

So great was his emotion that he could hardly frame the words. It seemed to him too good to be true, too like a beautiful dream, that this obese bimbo was about to become his uncle and so eligible for the Drones Club contest.

An embarrassed look had come into Kirk Rockaway's face. Again he hesitated before he spoke.

'No, we're not engaged.'

'You aren't?'

'Not yet. It's like this. She came to San Francisco a year or so ago.'

'Yes, I remember she went over to America. She's very fond of travelling.'

'We met at a dinner party. It was a Thanksgiving dinner with turkey, sweet potatoes, mince pie — the customary Thanksgiving menu. She sat opposite me, and the way she sailed into the turkey — enjoying it, *understanding* it, not picking at it as the other women were doing — hit me right here,' said Kirk Rockaway, touching the left side of his bulging waistcoat. 'And when I watched her handle the mince pie, I knew my fate was sealed. But I haven't actually proposed yet.'

'Why not?'

'I haven't the nerve.'

'What!'

'No, sir, I haven't the nerve.'

'Why not?'

'I don't know. I just haven't.'

A blinding light flashed upon Bingo. Mr. Purkiss's words rang in his ears. 'He is a lifelong teetotaller', Mr. Purkiss had said, and the whole thing became clear to him.

'Have you tried having a drink?' he asked.

'I've drunk a good deal of barley water.'

'Barley water!'

'But it seems to have no effect.'

'I'm not surprised. Barley water!' Bingo's voice was vibrant with scorn. 'What on earth's the good of barley water? How can you expect to be the masterful wooer on stuff like that? I should be a bachelor today if I hadn't had the prudence to fill myself to the brim with about a quart of mixed champagne and stout before asking Rosie to come registrar's-officing with me. That's what you want, champagne and stout. It'll make a new man of you.'

Kirk Rockaway looked dubious.

'But that's alcohol, and I promised my late mother I would never drink alcohol.'

'Well, I think if you could get in touch with her on the ouija board and explain the situation, making it clear that you needed the stuff for a good cause, she would skip the red tape and tell you to go to it. But that would take time. It might be hours before you got the connection. What you want is a noggin of it now, and then when you are nicely primed, we will go and drop in on my aunt. She has been away on a Mediterranean cruise, but she may be back by now. Waiter, bring us a bottle of Bollinger and all the stout you can carry.'

It was some half hour later that Kirk Rockaway looked across the table with a new light in his eyes. They had become reddish in colour and bulged a good deal. His diction, when he spoke, was a little slurred.

'Old man,' he said, 'I like your face.'

'Do you, old man?' said Bingo.

'Yes, old man, I do. And do you know why I like your face?'

'No, old man, I don't. Why do you like my face?'

'Because it is so different in every respect from Mortimer Frisby's.'

'Who is Mortimer Frisby?'

'You may well ask. He conducts the Children's Page on the *San Francisco Herald*, and calls himself a critic. Do you know what he said about my last book, old man?'

'No, what did he say, old man?'

'I'll tell you what he said. His words are graven on my heart and I quote verbatim. "We think," he said, "that Mr. Rockaway should not too lightly assume that all the children he writes for have water on the brain." How about that?'

'Monstrous!'

'Monstrous is right.'

'Abominable!'

'Abominable is correct.'

'The man must be mad.'

'Of course he is. But if he thinks he'll get off on a plea of insanity, he's very much mistaken. I propose to poke him in the snoot. We'll have just one more bottle for the road, and then I'll go and attend to it.'

'Where is he?'

'San Francisco.'

'You can't go to San Francisco.'

'Why not? I believe,' said Kirk Rockaway a little stiffly, 'that San Francisco is open for being gone to at about this time.'

'But it's such a long way. Besides, you were going to propose to my aunt.'

'Was I? Yes, by jove, you're right. It had slipped my mind.'

'Do it now. If you're feeling up to it.'

'I'm feeling great. I'm feeling strong, forceful, dominant. Do you know what I shall do that woman?'

'Bend her to your will?'

'Precisely. I shall stand no nonsense from her. Women are apt to want long engagements and wedding services with full choral effects, but none of that for me. We shall be married ... where was it you said you were married?'

'At the registrar's.'

'They give you quick service there?'

'Very quick. Over in a flash.'

'Then that's the place that gets my custom. And if I hear a yip out of her to the contrary, I shall poke her in the snoot. Come on, pay the check and let's go.'

Bingo's jaw fell.

'You mean pay the bill?'

'If that's what you like to call it.'

'But I thought you were standing me this dinner.'

'What ever gave you that silly idea?'

'You said you would because I was Rosie M. Banks's husband.'

'Whose husband?'

'Rosie M. Banks.'

'Never heard of her,' said Kirk Rockaway. 'It's your treat, so come across. Or would you prefer that I gave you a poke in the snoot?'

And his physique was so robust and his manner so intimidating that it seemed to Bingo that he had no alternative. With a groan that came up from the soles of his feet he felt in his pocket for Mr. Purkiss's ten pounds and with trembling finger beckoned to the waiter.

Bingo's aunt's house was in the Kensington neighbourhood, and thither they repaired in a taxi cab. It was a longish journey, but Kirk Rockaway enlived it with college yells remembered from earlier days. As they alighted, he was in the middle of one and he finished it while ringing the door bell.

The door opened. Willoughby appeared. Kirk Rockaway tapped him authoritatively on the chest and said:

'Take me to your leader!'

'Sir!'

'The Beenstock broad. I want a word with her.'

'Mrs. Beenstock is not at home, and I would be greatly obliged sir, if you would pop off.'

'I will not pop off. I demand to see the woman I love instantly,' thundered Kirk Rockaway, continuing to tap the butler like a woodpecker. 'There is a plot to keep her from me, and I may mention that I happen to know the ringleaders. If you do not immediately — '

He broke off, not because he had said his say but because he overbalanced and fell down the steps. Bingo, who had entered the hall, thought he saw him bounce twice, but he was in a state of great mental perturbation and may have been mistaken. Willoughby closed the front door, and Bingo wiped his forehead. His own forehead, not Willoughby's.

'Isn't my aunt at home?'

'No, sir. She returns tomorrow.'

'Why didn't you tell the gentleman that?'

'The gentleman was pie-eyed, Mr. Richard. Hark at him now.'

He was alluding to the fact that Kirk Rockaway was now banging on the door with the knocker, at the same time shouting in a stentorian voice that the woman he loved was being held incommunicado by a gang in the pay of Mortimer Frisby. Then abruptly the noise ceased and Bingo, peering through the little window at the side of the door, saw that the sweet singer of Oakland, San Francisco, was in conversation with a member of the police force. He was too far away to catch the gist of their talk, but it must have been acrimonious, for it had been in progress only a few moments when Kirk Rockaway, substituting action for words, hit the constable on the tip of the nose. The hand of the law then attached itself to his elbow and he was led away into the night.

The magistrate at Bow Street next morning took a serious view of the case. The tidal wave of lawlessness which was engulfing London, he said, must be checked and those who added fuel to its flames by punching policemen must be taught that they could not escape the penalty of their misdeeds.

'Fourteen days,' he said, coming to the point, and Bingo, who had attended the proceedings, tottered from the court feeling that this was the end. No hope now of that well-nourished man marrying his Aunt Myrtle in time to be entered for the Fat Uncles stakes. When the judging was done, he would still be in his prison cell — gnawed, Bingo hoped, for he was in bitter mood, by rats. The future looked dark to him. He recalled a poem in which there had occurred the line 'the night that covers me, black as the Pit from pole to pole', and he felt that if he had been asked to describe his general position at the moment, he could not have put the thing better himself. The words fitted his situation like the paper on the wall.

Only one ray of hope, and that a faint one, lightened his darkness. Willoughby had said that his aunt would be back from her Mediterranean cruise today, and he had sometimes found her responsive to the touch, if tactfully approached. It was a chance which Charles ('Charlie Always Pays') Pikelet would have estimated at perhaps 100 to 8, but it was a chance. He hastened to her house and pressed the front door bell.

'Good morning, Willoughby.'

'Good morning, Mr. Richard.'

'You and your Whistler's Mothers!'

'I would prefer not to dwell on that topic, sir.'

'So would I. Is my aunt in?'

'No, sir. They have gone out to do some shopping.'

'They?' said Bingo, surprised that the butler should have spoken of his employer, stout though she was, in the plural.

'Madam and Sir Hercules, Mr. Richard.'

'Who on earth is Sir Hercules?'

'Madam's husband, sir. Sir Hercules Foliot-Foljambe.'

'What!'

'Yes, sir. It appears that they were shipmates on the cruise from which Madam has just returned. I understand that the wedding took place in Naples.'

'Well, I'll be blowed. You never know what's going to happen next in these disturbed times, do you?'

'No, sir.'

'Of all the bizarre occurrences! What sort of a chap is he?'

'Bald, about the colour of a tomato ketchup, and stout.'

Bingo started.

'Stout?'

'Yes, sir.'

'How stout?'

'There is a photograph of the gentleman in Madam's boudoir, if you care to see it.'

'Let's go,' said Bingo. He was conscious of a strange thrill, but at the same time he was telling himself that he must not raise his hopes too high. Probably, judged by Drones standards, this new uncle of his would prove to be nothing special.

A minute later, he had reeled and a sharp cry had escaped his lips. He was looking, spellbound, at the photograph of a man so vast, so like a captive balloon, that Kirk Rockaway seemed merely pleasantly plump in comparison. A woman, he felt, even one as globular as his Aunt Myrtle, would have been well advised before linking her lot with his to consult her legal adviser to make sure that she was not committing bigamy.

A long sigh of ecstasy proceeded from him.

'Up from the depths!' he murmured. 'Up from the depths!'

'Sir?'

'Nothing, nothing. Just a random thought. I'm going to borrow this photograph, Willoughby.'

'Madam may be annoyed on discovering its absence.'

'Tell her she'll have it back this afternoon. I only want to show it to a man at the Drones,' said Bingo.

He was thinking of his coming interview with Oofy Prosser. If Oofy was prepared to meet his terms, he would let him have — say — twenty per cent of this certain winner, but he meant to drive a hard bargain.

* 7 *

George and Alfred

The little group of serious thinkers in the bar parlour of the Angler's Rest were talking about twins. A Gin and Tonic had brought the subject up, a cousin of his having recently acquired a couple, and the discussion had not proceeded far when it was seen that Mr. Mulliner, the Sage of the bar parlour, was smiling as if amused by some memory.

'I was thinking of my brother's sons George and Alfred,' he explained. 'They were twins.'

'Identical?' asked a Scotch on the Rocks.

'In every respect.'

'Always getting mistaken for each other, I suppose?'

They would have been, no doubt, if they had moved in the same circles, but their walks in life kept them widely separated. Alfred was a professional conjuror and spent most of his time in London, while George some years previously had gone to seek his fortune in Hollywood, where after various vicissitudes he had become a writer of additional dialogue on the staff of Jacob Schnellenhamer of the Colossal-Exquisite corporation.

The lot of a writer of additional dialogue in a Hollywood studio is not an exalted one — he ranks, I believe, just above a script girl and just below the man who works the wind machine — but any pity I might have felt for George for being one of the dregs was mitigated by the fact that I knew his position was only temporary, for on his thirtieth birthday, which would be occurring very shortly, he would be coming into possession of a large fortune left to him in trust by his godmother.

It was on Mr. Schnellenhamer's yacht that I met George again after an interval of several years. I had become friendly with Mr. Schnellenhamer on one of his previous visits to England, and when I ran into him one day in Piccadilly he told me he was just off to Monte Carlo to discuss some business matters with Sam Glutz of the Perfecto-Wonderful, who was wintering there, and asked me if I would care to come along. I accepted the invitation gratefully, and the first person I saw when I came on board was George.

I found him in excellent spirits, and I was not surprised, for he said he had reached the age of thirty a few days ago and would be collecting his legacy directly we arrived in Monaco.

'Your trustee is meeting you there?'

'He lives there. An old boy of the name of Bassinger.'

'Well, I certainly congratulate you, George. Have you made any plans?'

'Plenty. And the first is to stop being a Yes man.'

'I thought you were a writer of additional dialogue.'

'It's the same thing. I've been saying Yes to Schnellenhamer for three years, but no longer. A radical change of policy there's going to be. In the privacy of my chamber I've been practising saying No for days. No, Mr. Schnellenhamer. You're quite mistaken, Mr. Schnellenhamer. You're talking through your hat, Mr. Schnellenhamer. Would it be going too far if I told him he ought to have his head examined?'

'A little, I think.'

'Perhaps you're right.'

'You don't want to hurt his feelings.'

'I don't think he has any. Still, I see what you mean.'

We arrived in Monte Carlo after a pleasant voyage, and as soon as we had anchored in Monaco harbour I went ashore to see the sights and buy the papers, and I was thinking of returning to the yacht, when I saw George coming along, seeming to be in a hurry. I hailed him, and to my astonishment he turned out to be not George but Alfred, the last person I would have expected to find in Monte Carlo. I had always supposed that conjurors never left London except to appear at children's parties in the provinces.

He was delighted to see me. We had always been very close to one another. Many a time as a boy he had borrowed my top hat in order to take rabbits out of it, for even then he was acquiring the rudiments of his art and the skill which had enabled him to bill himself as The Great Alfredo. There was genuine affection in his manner as he now produced a hard-boiled egg from my breast pocket.

'But how in the world do you come to be here, Alfred?' I asked.

His explanation was simple.

'I'm appearing at the Casino. I have a couple of spots in the revue there, and I don't mind telling you that I'm rolling the customers in the aisles nightly,' he said, and I recalled that he had always interspersed his feats with humorous dialogue. 'How do you happen to be in Monte Carlo? Not on a gambling caper, I trust?'

'I am a guest on Mr. Schnellenhamer's yacht.'

He started at the mention of the name.

'Schnellenhamer? The movie man? The one who's doing the great Bible epic Solomon And The Queen of Sheba?'

'Yes, we are anchored in the harbour.'

'Well, well,' said Alfred. His air was pensive. My words had apparently started a train of thought. Then he looked at his watch and uttered an exclamation. 'Good Lord,' he said, 'I must rush, or I'll be late for rehearsal.'

And before I could tell him that his brother George was also on Mr. Schnellenhamer's yacht he had bounded off.

Mr. Schnellenhamer was on the deck when I reached the yacht, concluding a conversation with a young man whom I presumed to be a reporter, come to interview him. The young man left, and Mr. Schnellenhamer jerked a thumb at his retreating back.

'Listen,' he said. 'Do you know what that fellow's been telling me? You remember I was coming here to meet Sam Glutz? Well, it seems that somebody mugged Sam last night.'

'You don't say!'

'Yessir, laid him out cold. Are those the papers you've got there? Lemme look. It's probably on the front page.'

He was perfectly correct. Even George would have had to say 'Yes, Mr. Schnellenhamer.' The story was there under big headlines. On the previous night, it appeared, Mr. Glutz had been returning from the Casino to his hotel, when some person unknown had waylaid him and left him lying in the street in a considerably battered condition. He had been found by a passer-by and taken to the hospital to be stitched together.

'And not a hope of catching the fellow,' said Mr. Schnellenhamer.

I pointed out that the paper said that the police had a clue, and he snorted contemptuously.

'Police!'

'At your service,' said a voice, and turning I saw what I thought for a moment was General De Gaulle. Then I realised that he was some inches shorter than the General and had a yard or so less nose. But not even General De Gaulle could have looked sterner and more intimidating. 'Sergeant Brichoux of the Monaco police force,' he said. 'I have come to see a Mr. Mulliner, who I understand is a member of your entourage.'

This surprised me. I was also surprised that he should be speaking English so fluently, but the explanation soon occurred to me. A sergeant of police in a place like Monte Carlo; constantly having to question international spies, heavily veiled adventuresses and the like, would soon pick it up.

'I am Mr. Mulliner,' I said.

'Mr. George Mulliner?'

'Oh, George? No, he is my nephew. You want to see him?'

'I do.'

'Why?' asked Mr. Schnellenhamer.

'In connection with last night's assault on Mr. Glutz. The police have reason to believe that he can assist them in their enquiries.'

'How?'

'They would like him to explain how his wallet came to be lying on the spot where Mr. Glutz was attacked. One feels, does one not, that the fact is significant. Can I see him, if you please?' said Sergeant Brichoux, and a sailor was despatched to find George. He returned with the information that he did not appear to be on board.

'Probably gone for a stroll ashore,' said Mr. Schnellenhamer.

'Then with your permission,' said the sergeant, looking more sinister than ever, 'I will await his return.'

'And I'll go and look for him,' I said.

It was imperative, I felt, that George be intercepted and warned of what was waiting for him on the yacht. It was, of course, absurd to suppose that he had been associated in any way with last night's outrage, but if his wallet had been discovered on the scene of the crime, it was obvious that he would have a good deal of explaining to do. As I saw it, he was in the position the hero is always getting into in novels of suspense — forced by circumstances, though innocent, into the role of Suspect Number One and having a thoroughly sticky time till everything comes right in the last chapter.

It was on a bench near the harbour that I found him. He was sitting with his head between his hands, probably feeling that if he let go of it it would come in half, for when I spoke his name and he looked up, it was plain to see that he was in the grip of a severe hangover. I am told by those who know that there are six varieties of hangover — the Broken Compass, the Sewing Machine, the Comet, the Atomic, the Cement Mixer and the Gremlin Boogie, and his aspect suggested that he had them all.

I was not really surprised. He had told me after dinner on the previous night that he was just off to call on his trustee and collect his inheritance, and it was natural to suppose that after doing so he would celebrate. But when I asked him if this was so, he uttered one of those hollow rasping laughs that are so unpleasant.

'Celebrate!' he said. 'No, I wasn't celebrating. Shall I tell you what happened last night? I went to Bassinger's hotel and

gave my name and asked if he was in, and they told me he had
checked out a week or two ago and had left a letter for me. I
took the letter. I opened it. I read it. And having read it . . .
Have you ever been slapped in the eye with a wet fish?'

'Oddly enough, no.'

'I was once when I got into an argument with an angler down
at Santa Monica, and the sensation now was very similar. For
this letter, this *billet doux* from that offspring of unmarried
parents P. P. Bassinger, informed that he had been gambling
for years with the trust money and was deeply sorry to say that
there was now no trust. It had gone. So, he added, had he. By
the time I read this, he said, he would be in one of those broad-
minded South American countries where they don't believe in
extradition. He apologised profusely, but places the blame on
some man he had met in a bar who had given him an infallible
system for winning at the tables. And why my godmother gave
the trusteeship to someone living in Monte Carlo within easy
walking distance of the Casino we shall never know. Just asking
for it is the way it looks to me.'

My heart bled for him. By no stretch of optimism could I
regard this as his lucky day. All this and Sergeant Brichoux,
too. There was a quaver in my voice as I spoke.

'My poor boy!'

'Poor is right.'

'It must have been a terrible shock.'

'It was.'

'What did you do?'

'What would you have done? I went out and got pie-eyed.
And here's a funny thing I had the most extraordinary nightmare. Do you ever have nightmares?'

'Sometimes.'

'Bad ones?'

'Occasionally.'

'I'll bet they aren't as bad as the one I had. I dreamed that I
had done a murder. And that dream is still lingering with me. I
keep seeing myself engaged in a terrific brawl with someone
and laying him out. It's a most unpleasant sensation. Why are
you looking at me like a sheep with something on its mind?'

I had to tell him.

'It wasn't a nightmare, George.'

He seemed annoyed.

'Don't be an ass. Do you think I don't know a nightmare when I see one?'

'I repeat, it was no nightmare.'

He looked at me incredulously, his jaw beginning to droop like a badly set soufflé.

'You don't mean it actually happened?'

'I fear so. The papers have featured it.'

'I really slugged somebody?'

'Not just somebody. The president of a motion picture corporation, which makes your offence virtually *lèse majesté*.'

'Then how very fortunate,' said George, looking on the bright side after a moment of intense thought, 'that nobody can possibly know it was me. That certainly takes a weight off my mind. You're still goggling at me like a careworn sheep. Why is that?'

'I was thinking what a pity it was that you should have dropped your wallet — containing your name and address — on the spot of the crime.'

'Did I do that?'

'You did.'

'Hell's bells!'

'Hell's bells is correct. There's a sergeant of police on board the yacht now, waiting for your return. He has reason to believe that you can assist him in his enquiries.'

'Death and despair!'

'You may well say so. There is only one thing to be done. You must escape while there is yet time. Get over the frontier into Italy.'

'But my passport's on the yacht.'

'I could bring it to you.'

'You'd never find it.'

'Then I don't know what to suggest. Of course, you might — '

'That's no good.'

'Or you could — '

'That's no good either. No,' said George, 'this is the end. I'm a rat in a trap. I'm for it. Well-meaning, not to be blamed, the victim of the sort of accident that might have happened to anyone when lit up as I was lit, but nevertheless for it. That's Life. You come to Monte Carlo to collect a large fortune, all pepped

up with the thought that at last you're going to be able to say
No to old Schnellenhamer, and what do you get? No fortune, a
headache, and to top it all off the guillotine or whatever they
have in these parts. That's Life, I repeat. Just a bowl of cher-
ries. You can't win.'

Twin! I uttered a cry, electrified.

'I have it, George!'

'Well?'

'You want to get on the yacht.'

'Well?'

'To secure your passport.'

'Well?'

'Then go there.'

He gave me a reproachful look.

'If,' he said, 'You think this is the sort of stuff to spring on a
man with a morning head who is extremely worried because the
bloodhounds of the law are sniffing on his trail and he's liable to
be guillotined at any moment, I am afraid I cannot agree with
you. On your own showing that yacht is congested with sergeants of police, polishing the handcuffs and waiting eagerly
for my return. I'd look pretty silly sauntering in and saying
"Well, boys, here I am". Or don't you think so?'

'I omitted to mention that you would say you were Alfred.'

He blinked.

'Alfred?'

'Yes.'

'My brother Alfred?'

'Your twin brother Alfred,' I said, emphasising the second
word in the sentence, and I saw the light of intelligence creep
slowly into his haggard face. 'I will go there ahead of you and
sow the good seed by telling them that you have a twin brother
who is your exact double. Then you make your appearance.
Have no fear that your story will not be believed. Alfred is at
this moment in Monte Carlo, performing nightly in the revue at
the Casino and is, I imagine, a familiar figure in local circles.
He is probably known to the police — not, I need scarcely say,
in any derogatory sense but because they have caught his act and
may have been asked by him to take a card — any card — and
memorise it before returning it to the pack, his aim being to
produce it later from the inside of a lemon. There will be no

question of the innocent deception failing to succeed. Once on board it will be a simple matter to make some excuse to go below. An urgent need for bicarbonate of soda suggests itself. And once below you can find your passport, say a few graceful words of farewell and leave.'

'But suppose Schnellenhamer asks me to do conjuring tricks?'

'Most unlikely. He is not one of those men who are avid for entertainment. It is his aim in life to avoid it. He has told me that it is the motion picture magnate's cross that everybody he meets starts acting at him in the hope of getting on the payroll. He says that on a good morning in Hollywood he has sometimes been acted at by a secretary, two book agents, a life insurance man, a masseur, the man with the benzedrine, the studio watchman, a shoe shine boy and a barber, all before lunch. No need to worry about him wanting you to entertain him.'

'But what would be Alfred's reason for coming aboard?'

'Simple. He has heard that Mr. Schnellenhamer has arrived. It would be in the Society Jottings column. He knows that I am with Mr. Schnellenhamer —'

'How?'

'I told him so when I met him yesterday. So he has come to see me.'

The light of intelligence had now spread over George's face from ear to ear. He chuckled hoarsely.

'Do you know, I really believe it would work.'

'Of course it will work. It can't fail. I'll go now and start paving the way. And as your raiment is somewhat disordered, you had better get a change of clothes, and a shave and a wash and brush-up would not hurt. Here is some money,' I said, and with an encouraging pat on the back I left him.

Brichoux was still at his post when I reached the yacht, inflexible determination written on every line of his unattractive face. Mr. Schnellenhamer sat beside him looking as if he were feeling that what the world needed to make it a sweeter and better place was a complete absence of police sergeants. He had never been fond of policemen since one of them, while giving him a parking ticket, had recited Hamlet's To be or not to be speech to give him some idea of what he could do in a dramatic role. I proceeded to my mission without delay.

'Any sign of my nephew?' I asked.

'None,' said the Sergeant.

'He has not been back?'

'He has not.'

'Very odd.'

'Very suspicious.'

An idea struck me.

'I wonder if by any chance he has gone to see his brother.'

'Has he a brother?'

'Yes. They are twins. His name is Alfred. You have probably seen him, sergeant. He is playing in the revue at the Casino. Does a conjuring act.'

'The Great Alfredo?'

'That is his stage name. You have witnessed his performance?'

'I have.'

'Amazing the resemblance between him and George. Even I can hardly tell them apart. Same face, same figure, same way of walking, same coloured hair and eyes. When you meet George, you will be astounded at the resemblance.'

'I am looking forward to meeting Mr. George Mulliner.'

'Well, Alfred will probably be here this morning to have a chat with me, for he is bound to have read in the paper that I am Mr. Schnellenhamer's guest. Ah, here he comes now,' I said, as George appeared on the gangway. 'Ah, Alfred.'

'Hullo, uncle.'

'So you found your way here?'

'That's right.'

'My host, Mr. Schnellenhamer.'

'And Sergeant Brichoux of the Monaco police.'

'How do *you* do? Good morning, Mr. Schnellenhamer, I have been wanting very much to meet you. This is a great pleasure.'

I was proud of George. I had been expecting a show of at least some nervousness on his part, for the task he had undertaken was a stern one, but I could see no trace of it. He seemed completely at his ease, and he continued to address himself to Mr. Schnellenhamer without so much as a tremor in his voice.

'I have a proposition I would like to put up to you in connection with your forthcoming Bible epic Solomon And The

Queen Of Sheba. You have probably realised for yourself that the trouble with all these ancient history super-pictures is that they lack comedy. Colossal scenery, battle sequences of ten thousand a side, more semi-nude dancing girls than you could shake a stick at, but where are the belly laughs? Take *Cleopatra*. Was there anything funny in that? Not a thing. And what occurred to me the moment I read your advance publicity was that what Solomon And The Queen of Sheba needs, if it is really to gross grosses, is a comedy conjuror, and I decided to offer my services. You can scarcely require to be told how admirably an act like mine would fit into the scheme of things. There is nothing like a conjuror to keep a monarch amused through the long winter evenings, and King Solomon is bound to have had one at his court. So what happens? The Queen of Sheba arrives. The magnificence of her surroundings stuns her. "The half was not told unto me," she says. "You like my little place?" says the King. "Well, it's a home. But wait, you ain't seen nothing yet. Send for the Great Alfredo." And on I come. "Well, folks," I say, "a funny thing happened to me on my way to the throne room," and then I tell a story and then a few gags and then I go into my routine, and I would like just to run through it now. For my first trick — '

I was aghast. Long before the halfway mark of this speech the awful truth had flashed upon me. It was not George whom I saw before me — through a flickering mist — but Alfred, and I blamed myself bitterly for having been so mad as to mention Mr. Schnellenhamer to him, for I might have known that he would be inflamed by the news that the motion-picture magnate was within his reach and that here was his chance of getting signed up for a lucrative engagement. And George due to appear at any moment! No wonder that I reeled and had to support myself on what I believe is called a bollard.

'For my first trick,' said Alfred, 'I shall require a pound of butter, two bananas and a bowl of goldfish. Excuse me. Won't keep you long.'

He went below, presumably in quest of these necessaries, and as he did so George came up the gangway.

There was none of that breezy self-confidence in George which had so impressed me in Alfred. He was patently suffering from stage fright. His legs wobbled and I could see his adam's apple going up and down as if pulled by an invisible string. He looked like a nervous speaker at a public banquet who on rising to his feet to propose the toast of Our Guests realises that he has completely forgotten the story of the two Irishmen Pat and Mike, with which he had been hoping to convulse his audience.

Nor did I blame him, for Sergeant Brichoux had taken a pair of handcuffs from his pocket and was breathing on them and polishing them on his sleeve, while Mr. Schnellenhamer subjected him to the stony glare which had so often caused employees of his on the Colossal-Exquisite lot to totter off to the commissary to restore themselves with frosted malted milk shakes. There was an ominous calm in the motion picture magnate's manner such as one finds in volcanoes just before they erupt and make householders in the neighbourhood wish they had settled elsewhere. He was plainly holding himself in with a powerful effort, having decided to toy with my unhappy nephew before unmasking him for George's opening words had been 'Good morning. I — er — that is to say — I — er — my name is Alfred Mulliner', and I could see that neither on the part of Mr. Schnellenhamer or of Sergeant Brichoux was there that willing suspension of disbelief which dramatic critics are always writing about.

'Good morning,' said the former. 'Nice weather.'

'Yes, Mr Schnellenhamer.'

'Good for the crops.'

'Yes, Mr. Schnellenhamer.'

'Though bad for the umbrella trade.'

'Yes, Mr. Schnellenhamer.'

'Come along and join the party. Alfred Mulliner did you say the name was?'

'Yes, Mr. Schnellenhamer.'

'You lie!' thundered Mr. Schnellenhamer, unmasking his batteries with horrifying abruptness. 'You're no more Alfred Mulliner than I am, which isn't much. You're George Mulliner, and you're facing a murder rap or the next thing to it. Send for the police,' he said to Sergeant Brichoux.

'I *am* the police,' the sergeant reminded him, rather coldly it seemed to me.

'So you are. I was forgetting. Then arrest this man.'

'I will do so immediately.'

Sergeant Brichoux advanced on George handcuffs in hand, but before he could adjust them to his wrists an interruption occurred.

Intent though I had been on the scene taking place on the deck of the yacht, I had been able during these exchanges to observe out of the corner of my eye that a heavily bandaged man of middle age was approaching us along the quay, and he now mounted the gangway and hailed Mr. Schnellenhamer with a feeble 'Hi, Jake.'

So profuse were his bandages that one would hardly have expected his own mother to have recognized him, but Mr. Schnellenhamer did.

'Sam Glutz!' he cried. 'Well, I'll be darned. I thought you were in the hospital.'

'They let me out.'

'You look like Tutunkahmen's mummy, Sam.'

'So would you if you'd been belted by a hoodlum like I was. Did you read about it in the papers?'

'Sure. You made the front page.'

'Well, that's something. But I wouldn't care to go through an experience like that again. I thought it was the end. My whole past life flashed before me.'

'You can't have liked that.'

'I didn't.'

'Well, you'll be glad to hear, Sam, that we've got the fellow who slugged you.'

'You have? Where is he?'

'Right there. Standing by the gentleman with the handcuffs.'

George's head had been bowed, but now he happened to raise it, and Mr. Glutz uttered a cry.

'*You!*'

'That's him. George Mulliner. Used to work for the Colossal-Exquisite, but of course I've fired him. Take him to the cooler, sergeant.'

Every bandage on Mr. Glutz's body rippled like wheat beneath a west wind, and his next words showed that what had caused this was horror and indignation at the programme Mr. Schnellenhamer had outlined.

'Over my dead body!' he cried. 'Why, that's the splendid young man who saved my life last night.'

'What!'

'Sure. The hood was beating the tar out of me when he came galloping up and knocked him for a loop, and after a terrific struggle the hood called it a day and irised out. Proud and happy to meet you, Mr. Mulliner, I think I heard Jake say he'd fired you. Well, come and work for the Perfecto-Wonderful, and I shall be deeply offended if you don't skin me for a salary beyond the dreams of avarice. I'll pencil you in as vice-president with brevet rank as a cousin by marriage.'

I stepped forward. George was still incapable of speech.

'One moment, Mr. Glutz,' I said.

'Who are you?'

'George's agent. And there is just one clause in the contract which strikes me as requiring revision. Reflect, Mr. Glutz. Surely cousin by marriage is a poor reward for the man who saved your life?'

Mr. Glutz was visibly affected. Groping among the bandages, he wiped away a tear.

'You're right,' he said. 'We'll make it brother-in-law. And now let's go and get a bit of lunch. You, too,' he said to me, and I said I would be delighted. We left the boat in single file — first Mr. Glutz, then myself, then George, who was still dazed. The last thing I saw was Alfred coming on deck with his pound of butter and his two bananas. I seemed to detect on his face a slight touch of chagrin, caused no doubt by his inability to locate the bowl of goldfish so necessary to his first trick.

* 8 *

A Good Cigar is a Smoke

When Lancelot Bingley, the rising young artist, became engaged to Gladys Wetherby, the poetess, who in addition to her skill with the pen had the face and figure of the better type of pin-up girl and eyes of about the colour of the Mediterranean on a good day, he naturally felt that this was a good thing and one that should be pushed along. The sooner the wedding took place, in his opinion, the better it would be for all concerned. He broached the subject to her as they were tucking into the *poulet rôti au cresson* one evening at the Crushed Pansy, the restaurant with a soul.

'What I would suggest,' he said, 'if you haven't anything special on next week, is that we toddle round to the registrar's and encourage him to do his stuff. They tell me these registrar fellows make a very quick job of it. The whole thing wouldn't take more than ten minutes or so, and there we would be with it off our minds, if you see what I mean.'

To his consternation, instead of clapping her hands in girlish glee and telling him that he had struck the right note there, she shook her head.

'I'm afraid it's not so simple as that.'

'What's your problem?'

'I was thinking of Uncle Francis.'

'Whose Uncle Francis?'

'My Uncle Francis.'

'I didn't know you had an Uncle Francis.'

'He was my mother's brother. Colonel Pashley-Drake. You've probably heard of him.'

'Not a word. Nobody tells me anything.'

'He used to be a famous big game hunter.'

Lancelot frowned. He was not fond of big game hunters. His own impulse, if he had met a wapiti of a gnu or whatever it might be, would have been to offer it a ham sandwich from his luncheon basket, and the idea of plugging it with a repeating rifle, as this Pashley-Drake presumably did, revolted him.

'I'm not sorry we never ran across each other, then. I wouldn't have liked him.'

'Mother did. She looked up to him very much, and when she died she left him a chunk of money which he was to hand over to me when I married.'

'Excellent.'

'Not so excellent, because I am only to get it if he approves of the man I want to marry. And he won't approve of you.'

'Why not?'

'You're an artist.'

'What's wrong with artists?'

'Uncle Francis thinks they spend all their time having orgies in studios and painting foreign princesses sitting on leopard skins in the nude.'

'Uncle Francis is a fathead.'

'Very true. But he's the one who controls the cash.'

'And you feel he won't part?'

'The betting's against it.'

'Then let's do without it. I've plenty,' said Lancelot, who was more fortunate than most artists in having a nice private income.

Gladys shook her head. It seemed to him that she was always shaking her head tonight.

'No,' she said. 'I need the money, and I won't get married without it. I'm not going to be one of those pauper wives who have to come and plead brokenly with their husbands every time they want the price of a new hat. Some of my married friends tell me it sometimes takes fully half a pint of tears before their mate can be induced to disgorge the most trifling sum. I couldn't do it. My pride forbids it.'

And though Lancelot argued eloquently with her all through the *poulet rôti au cresson* course and later during the after-dinner coffee, she was not to be moved from her decision. It was a gloomy young artist who saw her home and then went off and got plastered in a series of pubs. What, he was asking himself, would the harvest be and where did he go from here? He tried to tell himself that this was a mere whim on her part, but the theory brought him little consolation. He knew only too well that she had a whim of iron.

His hangover on the following day precluded for a space all thought of anything except bicarbonate of soda, but even when several beakers of the refreshing fluid had built him up physically he was no nearer to being his customary carefree self, for anguish and despair took over and he sat brooding and listless in his studio, incapable of putting brush to canvas. If a nude princess had looked in wanting her portrait painted, he would have refused the commission without hesitation, pleading in excuse that he was not in the mood. All he could do in the way of alleviating the agony that seared his soul was to play the accordion, always his solace in times of stress, and he had worked his way through Over the Rainbow and was preparing to tackle Old Man River, when the door flew open and Gladys bounded in, her manner animated and eyes shining, it seemed to him from a quick glance, like twin stars.

'Put away that stomach Steinway, my Prince Charming,' she cried, 'and listen to me, for I bring news that will make you go dancing about London like a nautch girl. Guess what arrived by the morning post. A letter from Uncle Francis.'

Lancelot was unable to see why this should be considered a cause for rejoicing.

'Oh, yes?' he said, not attempting to share her enthusiasm.

'And what do you think he was writing about? He's asked me to find him an artist to paint his portrait, to be presented to the Explorers Club. You get the job.'

Lancelot blinked, still unenthusiastic. His head had begun to pain him again, and he could imagine nothing less agreeable than painting the portrait of a big game hunter who would probably want to be portrayed with a gun in his hand and a solar topee on his head, standing with one foot on a stuffed antelope.

'Me?' he said. 'Why me?'

'Don't you see what this means? You'll be closeted with him day after day, and if you can't fascinate him under those conditions, you're not the king among men I've always thought you. By the end of a couple of weeks you'll have got him so that he can deny you nothing. You then tell him we're going to get married and he gives you his blessing and reaches for his fountain pen and cheque book. Any questions?'

Lancelot's listlessness fell from him like a garment. Even though his mind was working slowly this morning he was able to see the merits of the scheme.

'None,' he said. 'It's terrific.'

'I knew you'd think so.'

'But —'

A thought had occurred to Lancelot. As an artist he belonged to the ultra-modern school, expressing himself most readily in pictures showing a sardine tin, two empty beer bottles, a bunch of carrots and a dead cat, the whole intended to represent Paris

In Springtime. He doubted his ability to work in another vein.

'Would I be any good at a portrait?'

'Good enough for a gaggle of explorers. All explorers have weak eyes through staring at the sunrise on the Lower Zambesi. They won't notice a thing.'

'Well, if you say so. Then what's the drill?'

'Uncle Francis has a house down at Bittleton in Sussex. You go there tomorrow with your paints and brushes. I'll phone him to be expecting you.'

Another thought struck Lancelot.

'I suppose I'm in for a thin time as regards meals. Don't big game hunters live on pemmican and native maize and that sort of thing?'

'Uncle Francis doesn't. He has the most sensational cook. Every dish a poem.'

'That sounds all right,' said Lancelot, brightening. Being an artist, he usually made do of an evening with the knuckle end of a ham or something out of a tin, but he was by no means incapable of appreciating good cooking and had often wished, when at the Crushed Pansy, that the *poulet rôti au cresson* had been a bit better *rôti*. 'I go tomorrow, you say?'

'Better perhaps the day after tomorrow. That'll give you time to mug up Uncle Francis's book, My Life With Rod and Gun, so that you can draw him out about the things he used to shoot. He gave me a copy at Christmas, when I was expecting at least a wrist watch.'

'That's how it goes,' said Lancelot sympathetically.

'Yes, that's life,' Gladys agreed. 'And the best offer I got from the secondhand book shop was three pence, so the volume is still on my shelves. You can come and fetch it this afternoon.'

'And I leave the day after tomorrow?'

'That's right. I'll come and see you off at the station.'

As Lancelot sat in his compartment waiting for the train to start and gazing at Gladys, who was standing on the platform, he was thinking how much he loved her and what a dreadful thought it was that they were to be separated like this for who knew how long. He was to learn almost immediately that there were other dreadful thoughts going around. She now gave utterance to one of them.

'Oh, by the way, angel,' she said, 'there's one other thing. I almost forgot to tell you. Uncle Francis is rabidly opposed to smoking.'

'He is?' said Lancelot, feeling that the more he heard of this uncle of hers, the less attractive a character he appeared to be.

'So of course you'll have to knock it off for the duration.'

A strong shudder shook Lancelot. He was a heavy smoker in spite of having two aunts who belonged to the Anti-Tobacco League and kept sending him pamphlets showing how disastrous for the health the practice was. His jaw fell a couple of notches, and he stared at her incredulously.

'Knock off smoking?' he gasped, wondering if he could have heard her correctly.

'That's right.'

'For weeks and weeks? I couldn't!'

'You couldn't, eh?'

'No, I couldn't.'

'Well, you'd jolly well better, or — '

'Or what?'

'Else,' said Gladys, and the train moved off.

It was one of those trains that have not become attuned to the modern spirit of speed and hustle, and as it sauntered through the sunlit countryside Lancelot had ample opportunity to turn over Gladys's parting words in his mind and examine them. And the more he did so, the less he liked the sound of them. Nor is this surprising. There are probably no words in the language which a lover more dislikes to hear on the lips of his loved one than those two words 'or else'. They have a sinister ring calculated to chill the hardiest.

He mused. One cannot say that he was standing at a man's crossroads, for he was sitting, but it was plain to him that he was confronted with the most serious dilemma of his lifetime. If, on the one hand, he obeyed her behest and refrained from smoking, every nerve in his body would soon be sticking out and starting to curl at the ends and the softest chirrup of the early bird attending to its worm outside his window would send him shooting up to the ceiling as if some fun-loving practical joker had exploded a bomb beneath his bed. He had once knocked off smoking for two or three days, and he knew what it was like.

If, however, on the other hand, he took a strong line and stoutly refused to keep away from the box of fifty excellent cigars which he had brought with him, what then? He knew very well what then. There would be for him no wedding bells or whatever registrars substitute for them. Gladys was as nearly as made no matter an angel in human shape, but she was inclined like so many girls who have what it takes, to be imperious and of a trend of mind to resent hotly anything in the nature of what might be called funny business. And that she would class as funny business a deliberate flouting of her orders was sickeningly clear to him. She would return the ring, his letters and what was left of the bottle of scent he had given her on her birthday within minutes of learning of his disobedience.

There flitted into his mind an insidious line from an old poem of Rudyard Kipling's. 'A woman is only a woman,' it ran, 'but a good cigar is a smoke', and for one awful moment he found himself feeling that Mr. Kipling had said a mouthful. Then he remembered Gladys's starlike eyes, her slender figure and the little freckle on the tip of her nose and was strong again. It was with the resolve that however great his sufferings he would retain her love that he alighted at Bittleton station and a short time later was meeting the man whose rugged features he was about to record on canvas.

They were features, particularly the three chins, of an undisguised opulence. and his body was in keeping with his face. Colonel Pashley-Drake was, in short, a stout man. Indeed, the thought flashed through Lancelot's mind that if he wanted to have himself painted full length, it would be necessary to send back to London for a larger canvas than any that he had brought with him. He knew from reading *My Life With Rod And Gun* that the Colonel, when hunting big game, had frequently hidden behind a tree. To conceal him in this the evening of his life only a Californian redwood would have served. And when later they sat together at the dinner table, he got an inkling as to how this obesity had come about.

The dinner was a long one and in every respect superb. It was plain to Lancelot from the first spoonful of soup that Gladys had well described his host's cook as sensational. The fish confirmed his view that she was a cook in a thousand. He mentioned this to the Colonel, and the latter, a look of holy ecstasy in his eye, agreed that Mrs. Potter — for such was the gifted woman's name — was at the very head of her profession. After that he did not speak very much, being otherwise occupied.

Coffee after the meal was served in a study or library, a large room tastefully decorated with the heads of various fauna which had had the misfortune to meet the other when he was out with his gun. As they seated themselves, the Colonel wheezed apologetically.

'I am afraid I cannot offer you a cigar,' he said, and Lancelot raised a deprecating hand.

'Had you done so,' he assured him, 'I should have been obliged to decline it, with thanks of course for the kind thought. I do not smoke. Smoking,' said Lancelot, remembering a pamphlet sent to him by one of his aunts, 'causes nervous dyspepsia, sleeplessness, headache, weak eyes, asthma, bronchitis, neurasthenia, rheumatism, lumbago, sciatica, loss of memory, falling out of hair and red spots on the skin. I wouldn't smoke so much as a cigarette to please a dying grandfather. My friends often rally me on what they consider my finicky objection to having red spots on my skin, but I remain firm.'

'You are very sensible,' said Colonel Pashley-Drake with such obvious approval that Lancelot felt that the task of fascinating him would prove even easier than Glady's had predicted. He looked forward to the moment — at no distant date — when he would have the old buster rolling on the floor with paws in the air like a tickled dachshund.

The love feast became intensified as the time went on. The Colonel was plainly delighted that Lancelot had derived such pleasure from his little book and spoke fluently and well on the subject of tigers he had met and what to do when confronted with a charging rhinoceros, together with many an anecdote about the selected portions of gnus, giraffes and the like which ornamented the walls. At long last he stifled a yawn and said he thought he would be turning in, and they parted in an atmosphere of the utmost cordiality.

The dinner, as has been said, had been a long and heavy one, and it had left Lancelot with a feeling of repletion which only fresh air could relieve, and before going to bed he felt the prudent thing to do was to take a half-hour stroll in the garden. He proceeded to do so, and what with the beauty of the night and the thinking of long loving thoughts of Gladys he exceeded the estimated time by a wide margin. It was some two hours later when the advisability of going to bed presented itself, and he made his way back to the house — only to discover when he reached it that in his absence some hidden hand had locked the front door.

It was a blow which might have crushed a weaker man, but Lancelot was resourceful and the idea of trying the back door occurred to him almost immediately. He found that, too, securely fastened, and it became evident that unless he was prepared to pass the remainder of the night in the open it would be necessary to break a window. This, as noiselessly as possible, he did and climbing through found himself in what from the smell he took to be the kitchen. And he was about to grope in the darkness in the hope of finding the door, when a voice spoke, a harsh guttural voice which jarred unpleasantly on his sensitive ear, though the most musical voice speaking at that moment would equally have given him the illusion that the top of his head had parted from its moorings. It said rather curtly:

'Who are you?'

Suavity, Lancelot felt, was what he must strive for.

'It's quite all right,' he said obsequiously. 'I was locked out.'

'Who are you?'

'My name is Lancelot Bingley. I am staying in the house. I am an artist. I am here to paint Colonel Pashley-Drake's portrait. I would not advise waking him now, but if you enquire of him in the morning, he will support my statement.'

'Who are you?'

Annoyance began to compete with Lancelot's embarrassment. If voices asked you questions, he felt, they might at least take the trouble to listen to you when you answered them. His manner took on a stiffness.

'I have already informed you in a perfectly frank manner that my name is Lancelot Bingley and that I am staying in the house in order to paint — '

'Have a nut,' said the voice, changing the subject.

Lancelot's teeth came together with a sharp click. Few things are more mortifying to a proud man than the discovery that he has been wasting his time being respectful to a parrot, and he burned with resentment and pique. Ignoring the bird's suggestion — in the circumstances ill-timed and lacking in taste — that he should scratch its head, he continued groping for the door and eventually found it.

After that everything was simple. Bounding silently up the stairs, he flung open the door of his room and not bothering to turn on the light flung himself on his bed. Or rather not precisely on the bed but on some squashy substance inside it which proved on investigation to be Colonel Pashley-Drake. Pardonably a little overwrought by his recent exchange of ideas with the parrot, he had mistaken the Colonel's room — first to the left along the corridor — for his own, which, he now remembered, was the second on the left along the corridor.

He lost no time in climbing off his host's stomach, on which he rightly supposed he had been nestling, but it was too late. The mischief had been done. The Colonel was plainly emotionally disturbed. He soliloquised for some moments in some native dialect which was strange to Lancelot.

'What the devil?' he enquired at length, dropping into English.

Inspiration descended on Lancelot.

'I came to ask you about the portrait. I was wondering if you wanted it full length or just head and shoulders,' he said, prudently omitting to explain why such a speculation was needed.

His room mate quivered like someone doing one of the modern dances.

'You woke me at this time of night to ask me *that*!'

'I thought it a point that should be settled.'

'No reason why you should come jumping on my stomach.'

'No, there,' Lancelot admitted, 'I perhaps went a little too far. I am sorry for that.'

'Not half as sorry as I am. I was dreaming of rogue elephants, and I thought one of them had sat down on me. Do you know what I'd have done if you had played a trick like that on me in the old days in West Africa? I'd have shot you like a dog.'

'Really?'

'I assure you. It is routine in West Africa.'

'Tell me about West Africa,' said Lancelot, hoping to mollify.

'To hell with West Africa,' said the Colonel. 'Get out of here, and consider yourself fortunate that you aren't as full of holes as a colander.'

Lancelot left the room feeling somewhat despondent. During dinner and after it he had flattered himself that he had made a good impression on his host, but something seemed to tell him that he had now lost ground.

And what, meanwhile, of Gladys Wetherby? Working on a sonnet next morning, she was conscious of a strange feeling of uneasiness and apprehension which made it hard for her to get the lines the right length. Ever since she had seen Lancelot off on the train she had been a prey to doubts and fears. She adored him with a passion which already had produced six sonnets, a ballade and about half a pound of vers libre, but all engaged girls have the poorest opinion of the intelligence of the men they are engaged to, and she had never wavered in her view that her loved one's IQ was about equal to that of a retarded child of seven. If there was a way of bungling everything down at Bittleton, he would, she was convinced, spring to the task, and it was only the fact that there seemed no way in which even he could bungle that had led her to entrust him with the mission which meant so much to them both. All he had to do was paint a portrait and while painting it exercise the charm she knew him to possess, and surely even Lancelot Bingley was capable of that.

Nevertheless she continued ill at ease, and it was with more anguish than surprise that she read the telegram which reached her shortly after lunch. It ran:

> Drop everything and come Bittleton immediately. Disaster stares eyeball and your moral support sorely needed. Love and kisses. Lancelot.

For some moments she stood congealed, her worst fears confirmed. Then, going to her bedroom, she packed a few necessaries in a suitcase, and hailed a taxi. Twenty minutes later she was on the train, a ticket to Bittleton in her bag, and an hour and forty-five minutes after that she entered her uncle's garden. The first thing she saw there was Lancelot pacing up and down, his manner indistinguishable from that of a cat on hot bricks. He came tottering towards her.

'Thank heaven you're here,' he cried. 'I need your woman's intelligence. Perhaps you can tell me what to do for the best, for the storm clouds are lowering. I seem to remember saying in my telegram that disaster stared me in the eyeball. That in no way overstated it. Let me tell you what's happened.'

Gladys was staring at him dumbly. She had been expecting the worst, and this was apparently what she was going to get. If she had had any tan, she would have paled beneath it.

'Here, then, are the facts. I must begin by saying that last night I jumped on your uncle's stomach.'

'Jumped on his stomach?' whispered Gladys, finding speech.

'Oh, purely inadvertently, but I could tell by his manner that he was annoyed. It was like this,' said Lancelot, and he related briefly the events of the previous night. 'But that wouldn't have mattered so much,' he went on, 'if it hadn't been for what happened this morning. I had sauntered out into the garden with my after breakfast cigar — '

He paused. He thought he had heard a stepped-on cat utter a piercing yowl. But it was only Gladys commenting on what he had said. Her eyes, which under the right conditions could be so soft and loving, were shooting flames.

'I told you you were not to smoke!'

'I know, I know, but I thought it would be all right if no one saw me. One must have one's smoke after breakfast, or what are breakfasts for? Well, as I was saying, I sauntered out and lit up, and I hadn't puffed more than a few puffs when I heard voices.'

'Oh, heavens!'

'That, or something like it, was what I said, and I dived into the shrubbery. The voices came nearer. Someone was approaching, or rather I should have said that two persons were approaching, for if there had been only one person approaching, he would hardly have been talking to himself. Though of course, you do get that sort of thing in Shakespeare. Hamlet, to take but one instance, frequently soliloquised.'

'Lancelot!'

'My angel?'

'Get on with it.'

'Certainly, certainly. Where was I?'

'You were smoking your cigar, which I had expressly forbidden you to do, in the shrubbery.'

'No, there you are wrong. I was in the shrubbery, yes, but I was not smoking my cigar, and I'll tell you why. In my natural perturbation at hearing these voices and realising that two persons were approaching I had dropped it on the lawn.'

He paused again. Once more Gladys had uttered that eldrich scream so like in its timbre to that of a domestic cat with a number eleven boot on its tail.

'Lancelot Bingley, you ought to be in a padded cell!'

'Yes, yes, but don't keep interrupting me, darling, or I shall lose the thread. Well, these two approaching persons had now drawn quite close to where I lurked behind a laurel bush, and I was enabled to hear their conversation. One of them was your uncle, the other a globular woman whom I assumed to be the Mrs. Potter of whom I had heard so much, for she was sketching out the menu for tonight's dinner, which I don't mind telling you is going to be a pippin. Your uncle evidently thought so too, for he kept saying 'Excellent, excellent' and things like that, and my mouth was watering freely when all of a sudden a female shriek or cry rent the air and peeping cautiously round my laurel bush I saw the Potter female was pointing in an aghast sort of way at something lying on the grass and, to cut a long story short, it was my *cigar*.'

A dull despair weighed Gladys Wetherby down.

'So they caught you?' she said tonelessly.

'No,' said Lancelot, 'I lurked unseen. And of course they didn't know it was my cigar. I gathered from their remarks that the prime suspects are the chauffeur and the gardener. It naturally didn't occur to your uncle to pin the rap on me, because after dinner last night I had convinced him that I was a total abstainer.'

Indignation brought a flush to Gladys's face. No girl likes to be dragged into the depths of the country on a hot afternoon by a telegram from her betrothed saying that disaster stares him in eyeball when apparently disaster has been doing nothing of the sort.

'Then what's all the fuss about?' she demanded. 'Why the urgent S O S's? You're in the clear.'

Lancelot corrected her gently.

'No, my loved one. In the soup, yes, but not in the clear.'

'I don't understand you.'

'You will in about two seconds flat. I am sorry to have to add that on the advice of Mrs. Potter your uncle is having the cigar finger-printed.'

'What!'

'Yes. It appears that she has a brother or cousin or something at Scotland Yard, and she said that that was always the first thing they did with a piece of evidence. Taking the dabs, I believe they call it. So your uncle said he would lock it in his desk till it could be examined by the proper experts, and he picked it up carefully with his handkerchief, like they do in books. So now you see why that telegram of mine expressed itself so strongly. My fingerprints must be all over the damn thing, and it won't take those experts five minutes to lay the crime at my door.'

An expletive which she had picked up at the Poets Club in Bloomsbury burst from Gladys's lips. She clutched her brow.

'Don't talk,' she said. 'I want to think.'

She stood motionless, her brain plainly working at its maximum speed. A fly settled on her left eyebrow, but she ignored it. Lancelot watched her anxiously.

'Anything stirring?' he asked.

Glady's came out of her reverie.

'Yes,' she said, and her voice had lost its dull despondency. 'I see what to do. We must sneak down tonight when everyone's in bed and retrieve that cigar. I know where to find a duplicate key to Uncle Francis's desk. I used it a lot in my childhood when he kept chocolates there. Expect me at your bedroom door at about midnight, and we'll get cracking.'

'You think we can do it?'

'It'll be as easy as falling off a log,' said Gladys.

All artists are nervous, highly strung men, and Lancelot, as he waited for the girl he loved to come and tell him that zero hour had arrived, was not at his most debonair and carefree. The thought of the impending expedition had the worst effect on his morale. It so happened that for one reason or another he had never fallen off a log, but he assumed it to be a feat well within the scope of the least gifted, and why Gladys should think it resembled the hideous task that lay before them he could not imagine. He could tot up a dozen things that could go wrong. Suppose, to take an instance at random, the parrot overheard them and roused the house.

But when Gladys did appear, something of confidence returned to him. The mere look of her was encouraging. There is nothing that so heartens a man in a crisis as the feeling that he has a woman of strong executive qualities at his side. Macbeth, it will be remembered, had this experience.

'Sh!' said Gladys, though he had not spoken, and before they set out she had a word of advice on strategy and tactics to impart.

'Now listen, Lancelot,' she said. 'We want to conduct this operation with a minimum of sound effects. Your impulse, I know, will be to trip over your feet and fall downstairs with a noise like the delivery of a ton of coal, but resist it. Play the scene quietly. Okay? Right. Then let's go.'

Nothing marred the success of the expedition from the outset. True, Lancelot tripped over his feet as anticipated, but a quick snatch at the banisters enabled him to avoid giving the impersonation of the delivery of a ton of coals against which she had warned him. In silence they descended the stairs and stole noiselessly into the study. Gladys produced her duplicate key, and Lancelot was just saying to himself that if he were a bookie he would estimate the odds on the happy ending as at least four to one, when there occurred one of those unforeseen hitches which cannot be budgeted for. Even as Gladys, key in hand approached the desk there came from outside the sound of stealthy footsteps, and it was only too evident that their objective was the study in which they were trapped.

It was a moment fraught with embarrassment for the young couple, but each acted with a promptitude deserving of the highest praise. By the time the door opened no evidence of their presence was discernible, Gladys was concealed behind the curtains that draped the french windows, while Lancelot, having cleared the desk with a lissom bound, was crouching behind it, doing his best not to breathe.

The first sound he heard after the opening of the door was the click of key in a lock. It was followed by the scratching of a match, and suddenly there floated to his nostrils the unmistakable scent of cigar smoke. And even as he sought faintly for a solution of this mystery the curtains parted with a rattle and he was able to catch a glimpse of the upper portions of his betrothed. She was staring accusingly down at something beyond his range of vision, and when a sharp exclamation in Swahili broke the silence, he knew that this must be Colonel Pashley-Drake.

'So!' said Gladys.

There are not many good things one can say in answer to the word 'So!', especially if one is called upon to find one at a moment's notice, and the Colonel remained silent for a space. It was only when Gladys had repeated the word that he spoke.

'Ah, my dear,' he said, 'There you are. Sorry to have seemed a bit taciturn, but your abrupt appearance surprised me. I thought you were in bed and asleep. Well, no doubt it seems odd to you to find me here, but I can explain, and you will see how I am situated.'

'You are situated in an armchair with a whacking great cigar in your mouth, and I shall be glad to have the inside story.'

'You shall have it at once, and I think it will touch your heart. You were away from home, I believe, when Mrs. Potter entered my service?'

'She had been here a year when I first saw her.'

'So I thought. She was in the employment of a friend of mine when I was introduced to her superlative cooking. When he conked out — apoplexy, poor fellow, brought on, I have always felt, by over-indulgence in her steak and kidney pies — I immediately asked her to come to me, and I was stunned when she enquired if I was a non-smoker, adding that she held smoking to be the primary cause of all human ills and would never consider serving under the banner of an employer who indulged in the revolting practice. You follow me so far?'

'I get the picture.'

'It was a tricky situation, you will admit. On the one hand, I loved cigars. On the other, I adored good food. Which to choose? The whole of that night I lay sleepless on my bed, pondering, and when morning came I knew what my decision must be. I made the great sacrifice. But this morning the chauffeur or somebody dropped this cigar on the lawn, and the sight of it shook me to my depths. I had not seen one for three years, and all the old craving returned. Unable to resist the urge, I crept down here and . . . Well, that is the story, my dear, and I am sure you will not let this little lapse of mine come to Mrs. Potter's ears. I can rely on you?'

'Of course.'

'Thank you, thank you. You have taken a great weight off my mind. Bless my soul, I haven't felt so relieved since the afternoon in West Africa when a rhinoceros, charging on me with flashing eyes, suddenly sprained an ankle and had to call the whole thing off. I shudder to think what would have happened if Mrs. Potter had learned of my doings this night. She would have been off like a jack rabbit. I wouldn't have been able to see her for dust. She would have vanished like a dream at daybreak. But provided you seal your lips — '

'Oh, I'll seal them.'

'Thank you, my dear. I knew I could rely on you.'

'And you on your side will write a cheque for that bit of cash of mine. You see, I want to get married.'

'You do? Who to?'

'You know him. Lancelot Bingley.'

A hoarse exclamation in some little known Senegambian dialect burst from the Colonel's lips.

'You mean that artist fellow?'

'That's right.'

'You're joking.'

'I am not.'

'You mean you seriously intend to marry that pop-eyed young slab of damnation?'

'He is not pop-eyed.'

'But you will concede that he is a slab of damnation?'

'I will do nothing of the sort. Lancelot is a baa-lamb.'

'A baa-lamb?'

'Yes, a baa-lamb.'

'Well, he doesn't look to me like a baa-lamb. More like something the cat brought in, and not a very fastidious cat at that.'

In his nook behind the desk Lancelot flushed hotly. For a

moment he thought of rising to his feet with a curt 'I resent that remark', but prudence told him it was better not to interrupt.

'And it is not only his looks I object to,' continued the Colonel. 'I suppose he has kept it from you, but he goes about jumping on people's stomachs.'

'Yes, he mentioned that to me.'

'Well, then. You don't expect me to abet you in your crazy scheme of marrying a chap like that. I won't give you a penny.'

'Then I'll tell Mrs. Potter you're a secret smoker.'

The Colonel gasped. The cigar fell from his hand. He picked it up, dusted it and returned it to his lips. His voice, when he spoke, was hoarse and trembled.

'This is blackmail!'

'With the possible exception of diamonds,' said Gladys, 'a girl's best friend.'

Silence fell. The Colonel's eyes were strained and black. His chins vibrated. It was plain that he was engaged in serious thought. But the clash of wills could have but one ending.

'Very well,' he said at length, 'I consent. I do it with the utmost reluctance, for the idea of you marrying that . . . that . . . how shall I describe him . . . well, never mind, you know what I mean . . . chills me to the marrow. But I have no alternative. I cannot do without Mrs. Potter's cooking.'

'You shall have it.'

'And furthermore,' said Lancelot, shooting up from behind the desk and causing the Colonel to quiver like a smitten jelly, 'you shall have all the cigars you want. I have a box of fifty — or, rather, forty-nine — upstairs in my room and I give them to you freely. And after breakfast tomorrow I will show you a spot in the shrubbery where you can smoke your head off without fear of detection.'

The Colonel drew a deep breath. His eyes glowed with a strange light. His chins vibrated again, but this time with ecstasy. He said a few words in Cape Dutch, then, seeing that his companions had missed the gist, he obligingly translated.

'Gladys,' he said, 'I could wish you no better husband. He is, as you were telling me, one of the baa-lambs and in my opinion by no means the worst of them. I think you will be very happy.'

* 9 *

Sleepy Time

In his office on the premises of Popgood and Grooly, publishers of the Book Beautiful, Madison Avenue, New York, Cyril Grooly, the firm's junior partner, was practising putts into a tooth glass and doing rather badly even for one with a twenty-four handicap, when Patricia Binstead, Mr Popgood's secretary, entered, and dropping his putter he folded her in a close embrace. This was not because all American publishers are warmhearted impulsive men and she a very attractive girl, but because they had recently become betrothed. On his return from his summer vacation at Paradise Valley, due to begin this afternoon, they would step along to some convenient church and become man, if you can call someone with a twenty-four handicap a man, and wife.

'A social visit?' he asked, the embrace concluded, 'Or business?'

'Business. Popgood had to go out to see a man about subsidiary rights, and Count Dracula has blown in. Well, when I say Count Dracula, I speak loosely. He just looks like him. His name is Professor Pepperidge Farmer, and he's come to sign his contract.'

'He writes books?'

'He's written one. He calles it Hypnotism As A Device To Uncover The Unconscious Drives and Mechanism In An Effort To Analyse The Functions Involved Which Give Rise To Emotional Conflicts In The Waking State, but the title's going to be changed to Sleepy Time. Popgood thinks it's snappier.'

'Much snappier.'

'Shall I send him in?'

'Do so, queen of my soul.'

'And Popgood says Be sure not to go above two hundred dollars for the advance,' said Patrica, and a few moments later the visitor made his appearance.

It was an appearance, as Patricia had hinted, of a nature to chill the spine. Sinister was the adjective that automatically sprang to the lips of those who met Professor Pepperidge Farmer for the first time. His face was gaunt and lined and grim, and as his burning eyes bored into Cyril's the young publisher was conscious of a feeling of relief that this encounter was not taking place down a dark alley or in some lonely spot in the country. But a man used to mingling with American authors, few of whom look like anything on earth, is not readily intimidated and he greeted him with his customary easy courtesy.

'Come right in,' he said. 'You've caught me just in time. I'm off to Paradise Valley this afternoon.'

'A golfing holiday?' said the Professor, eyeing the putter.

'Yes, I'm looking forward to getting some golf.'

'How is your game?'

'Horrible,' Cyril was obliged to confess. 'Mine is a sad and peculiar case. I have the theory of golf at my fingertips, but once out in the middle I do nothing but foozle.'

'You should keep your head down.'

'So Tommy Armour tells me, but up it comes.'

'That's Life.'

'Or shall we say hell?'

'If you prefer it.'

'It seems the mot juste. But now to business. Miss Binstead tells me you have come to sign your contract. I have it here. It all appears to be in order except that the amount of the advance has not been decided on.'

'And what are your views on that?'

'I was thinking of a hundred dollars. You see,' said Cyril, falling smoothly into his stride, 'a book like yours always involves a serious risk for the publisher owing to the absence of the Sex Motif, which renders it impossible for him to put a nude female of impressive vital statistics on the jacket and no hope of getting banned in Boston. Add the growing cost of paper and the ever-increasing demands of printers, compositors, binders and . . . why are you waving your hands like that?'

'I have French blood in me. On the mother's side.'

'Well, I wish you wouldn't. You're making me sleepy.'

'Oh, am I? How very interesting. Yes, I can see that your

eyes are closing. You are becoming drowsy. You are falling
asleep ... you are falling asleep ... asleep ... asleep ...
asleep ...'

It was getting on for lunchtime when Cyril awoke. When he
did so, he found that the recent gargoyle was no longer with
him. Odd, he felt, that the fellow should have gone before they
had settled the amount of his advance, but no doubt he had
remembered some appointment elsewhere. Dismissing him
from his mind, Cyril resumed his putting, and soon after lunch
he left for Paradise Valley.

On the subject of Paradise Valley the public relations rep-
resentative of the Paradise Hotel has expressed himself very
frankly. It is, he says in his illustrated booklet, a dream world
of breath-taking beauty, and its noble scenery, its wide open
spaces, its soft mountain breezes and its sun-drenched pleas-
ances impart to the jaded city worker a new vim and vigour
and fill him so full of red corpuscles that before a day has
elapsed in these delightful surroundings he is conscious of a *je
ne sais quoi* and a *bien être* and goes about with his chin up and
both feet on the ground, feeling as if he had just come back
from the cleaner's. And, what is more, only a step from the
hotel lies the Squashy Hollow golf course, of whose amenities
residents can avail themselves on payment of a green fee.

What, however, the booklet omits to mention is that the
Squashy Hollow course is one of the most difficult in the
country. It was constructed by an exiled Scot who, probably
from some deep-seated grudge against the human race, had
modelled the eighteen holes on the nastiest and most repellent
of his native land, so that after negotiating — say — the Alps at
Prestwick the pleasure-seeker finds himself confronted by the
Stationmaster's Garden at St. Andrew's, with the Eden and
the Redan just around the corner.

The type of golfer it attracts, therefore, is the one with high
ideals and an implicit confidence in his ability to overcome the
toughest obstacles; the sort who plays in amateur cham-
pionships and mutters to himself 'Why this strange weakness?'
if he shoots worse than a seventy-five, and one look at it gave
Cyril that uncomfortable feeling known to scientists as the
heeby-jeebies. He had entered for the medal contest which was

to take place tomorrow, for he always entered for medal contests, never being able to forget that he had once shot a ninety-eight and that this, if repeated, would with his handicap give him a sporting chance of success. But the prospect of performing in front of all these hardened experts created in him the illusion that caterpillars to the number of about fifty-seven were parading up and down his spinal cord. He shrank from exposing himself to their bleak contemptuous stares. His emotions when he did would, he knew, be similar in almost every respect to those of a mongrel which has been rash enough to wander into some fashionable Kennel Show.

As, then, he sat on the porch of the Paradise Hotel on the morning before the contest, he was so far from being filled with *bien être* that he could not even achieve *je ne sais quoi*, and at this moment the seal was set on his despondency by the sight of Agnes Flack.

Agnes Flack was a large young woman who on the first day of his arrival had discovered that he was a partner in a publishing firm and had immediately begun to speak of a novel which she had written and would be glad to have his opinion of when he had a little time to spare. And experience had taught him that when large young women wrote novels they were either squashily sentimental or so Chatterleyesque that it would be necessary to print them on asbestos, and he had spent much of his leisure avoiding her. She seemed now to be coming in his direction, so rising hastily he made on winged feet for the bar. Entering in at a rapid gallop, he collided with a solid body, and this proved on inspection to be none other than Professor Pepperidge Farmer, looking more sinister than ever in Bermuda shorts, a shirt like a Turner sunset and a Panama hat with a pink ribbon round it.

He stood amazed. There was, of course, no reason why the other should not have been there, for the hotel was open to all whose purses were equal to the tariff, but somehow he seemed out of place, like a ghoul at a garden party or a vampire bat at a picnic.

'You!' he exclaimed. 'Whatever became of you that morning?'

'You allude to our previous meeting?' said the Professor. 'I saw you had dozed off, so I tiptoed out without disturbing you. I thought it would be better to resume our acquaintance in these more agreeable surroundings. For if you are thinking that my presence here is due to one of those coincidences which are so strained and inartistic, you are wrong. I came in the hope that I might be able to do something to improve your golf game. I feel I owe you a great deal.'

'You do? Why?'

'We can go into that some other time. Tell me, how is the golf going? Any improvement?'

If he had hoped to receive confidences, he could not have put the question at a better moment. Cyril did not habitually bare his soul to comparative strangers, but now he found himself unable to resist the urge. It was as though the Professor's query had drawn a cork and brought all his doubts and fears and inhibitions foaming out like ginger pop from a ginger pop bottle. As far as reticence was concerned, he might have been on a psychoanalyst's couch at twenty-five dollars the half hour. In burning words he spoke of the coming medal contest, stressing his qualms and the growing coldness of his feet, and the Professor listened attentively, clicking a sympathetic tongue from time to time. It was plain that though he looked like something Charles Addams might have thought up when in the throes of a hangover, if Mr. Addams does ever have hangovers, he had a feeling heart.

'I'm paired with a fellow called Sidney McMurdo, who they tell me is the club champion, and I fear his scorn. It's going to take me at least a hundred and fifteen shots for the round, and on each of those hundred and fifteen shots Sidney McMurdo will look at me as if I were something slimy and obscene that had crawled out from under a flat stone. I shall feel like a crippled leper, and so,' said Cyril, concluding his remarks, 'I have decided to take my name off the list of entrants. Call me weak if you will, but I can't face it.'

The Professor patted him on the shoulder in a fatherly manner and was about to speak, but before he could do so Cyril heard his name paged and was told that he was wanted on the telephone. It was some little time before he returned, and when he did the dullest eye could see that something had occurred to ruffle him. He found Professor Farmer sipping a lemon squash, and when the Professor asked him if he would care for one of the same, he thundered out a violent No.

'Blast and damn all lemon squashes!' he cried vehemently. 'Do you know who that was on the phone? It was Popgood, my senior partner. And do you know what he said? He wanted to know what had got into me to make me sign a contract giving you five thousand dollars advance on that book of yours. He said you must have hypnotised me.'

A smile probably intended to be gentle, but conveying the impression that he was suffering from some internal disorder, played over the Professor's face.

'Of course I did, my dear fellow. It was one of the ordinary business precautions an author has to take. The only way to get a decent advance from a publisher is to hypnotise him. That was what I was referring to when I said I owed you a great deal. But for you I should never have been able to afford a holiday at a place like Paradise Valley where even the simplest lemon squash sets you back a prince's ransom. Was Popgood annoyed?'

'He was.'

'Too bad. He should have been rejoicing to think that his money had been instrumental in bringing a little sunshine into a fellow creature's life. But let us forget him and return to this matter of your golfing problems.'

He had said the one thing capable of diverting Cyril's thoughts from his incandescent partner. No twenty-four handicap man is ever deaf to such an appeal.

'You told me you had all the theory of the game at your finger-tips. Is that so? Your reading has been wide?'

'I've read every golf book that has been written.'

'You mentioned Tommy Armour. Have you studied his preachings?'

'I know them by heart.'

'But lack of confidence prevents you putting them into practise?'

'I suppose that's it.'

'Then the solution is simple. I must hypnotise you again. You should still be under the influence, but the effects may have worn off and it's best to be on the safe side. I will instil into you the conviction that you can knock spots off the proudest McMurdo. When you take club in hand, it will be with the certainty that your ball is going to travel from Point A to

Point B by the shortest route and will meet with no mis-adventures on the way. Whose game would you prefer yours to resemble? Arnold Palmer's? Gary Player's? Jack Nicklaus's? Palmer's is the one I would recommend. Those spectacular finishes of his. You agree? Palmer it shall be, then. So away we go. Your eyes are closing. You are feeling drowsy. You are falling asleep . . . asleep . . . asleep . . .'

Paradise Valley was at its best next day, its scenery just as noble, its mountain breezes just as soft, its spaces fully as wide and open as the public relations man's booklet had claimed them to be, and Cyril, as he stood beside the first tee of the Squashy Hollow course awaiting Sidney McMurdo's arrival, was feeling, as he had confided to the caddy master when picking up his clubs, like a million dollars. He would indeed scarcely have been exaggerating if he had made it two million. His chin was up, both his feet were on the ground, and the red corpuscles of which the booklet had spoken coursed through his body like students rioting in Saigon, Moscow, Cairo, Panama and other centres. Professor Farmer, in assuring him that he would become as confident as Arnold Palmer, had understated it. He was as confident as Arnold Palmer, Gary Player, Ray Venturi, Jack Nicklaus and Tony Lema all rolled into one.

He had not been waiting long when he beheld a vast expanse of man approaching and presumed that this must be his partner for the round. He gave him a sunny smile.

'Mr. McMurdo? How do you do? Nice day. Very pleasant, those soft mountain breezes.'

The newcomer's only response was a bronchial sound such as might have been produced by an elephant taking its foot out of a swamp in a teak forest. Sidney McMurdo was in dark and sullen mood. On the previous night Agnes Flack, his fiancée, had broken their engagement owing to a trifling disagreement they had had about the novel she had written. He had said it was a lot of prune juice and advised her to burn it without delay, and she had said it was not, too, a lot of prune juice, adding that she never wanted to see or speak to him again, and this had affected him adversely. It always annoyed him when Agnes Flack broke their engagement, because it made him overswing, particularly off the tee.

He did so now, having won the honour, and was pained to see that his ball, which he had intended to go due north, was travelling nor'-nor'-east. And as he stood scowling after it, Cyril spoke.

'I wonder if you noticed what you did wrong there, Mr. McMurdo,' he said in the friendliest way. 'Your backswing was too long. Length of backswing does not have as much effect on distance as many believe. You should swing back only just as far as you can without losing control of the club. Control is all-important. I always take my driver to about the horizontal position on the back swing. Watch me now.'

And so saying Cyril with effortless grace drove two hundred and eighty yards down the fairway.

'See what I mean?' he said.

It was on the fourth green, after he had done an eagle, that he spoke again. Sidney McMurdo had had some difficulty in getting out of a sand trap and he hastened to give him the benefit of his advice. There was nothing in it for him except the glow that comes from doing an act of kindness, but it distressed him to see a quite promising player like McMurdo making mistakes of which a wiser head could so easily cure him.

'You did not allow for the texture of the sand,' he said. 'Your sand shot should differ with the texture of the sand. If it is wet, hard or shallow, your clubhead will not cut into it as deeply as it would into soft and shifting sand. If the sand is soft, try to dig into it about two inches behind the ball, but when it is hard penetrate it about one and a half inches behind the ball. And since firm sand will slow down your club considerably, be sure to give your swing a full follow-through.'

The game proceeded. On the twelfth Cyril warned his partner to be careful to remember to bend the knees slightly for greater flexibility through the swing, though — on the sixteenth — he warned against bending them too much, as this often led to topping. When both had holed out at the eighteenth, he had a word of counsel to give on the subject of putting.

'Successful putting, Sidney,' he said, for he felt that they might now consider themselves on first name terms. 'Depends largely on the mental attitude. Confidence is everything. Never let anxiety make you tense. Never for an instant harbour the thought that your shot may miss. When I sank that last fifty-foot putt, I *knew* it was going in. My mind was filled with a picture of the ball following a proper line to the hole, and it is that sort of picture I should like to encourage in you. Well, it has been a most pleasant round. We must have another soon. I shot a sixty-two, did I not? I thought so. I was quite on my game today, quite on my game.'

Sidney McMurdo's eyebrows, always beetling, were beetling still more darkly as he watched Cyril walking away with elastic tread. He turned to a friend who had just come up.

'Who is that fellow?' he asked hoarsely.

'His name's Grooly,' said the friend. 'One of the summer visitors.'

'What's his handicap?'

'I can tell you that, for I was looking at the board this morning. It's twenty-four.'

'Air!' cried Sidney McMurdo, clutching his throat. 'Give me air!'

Cyril, meanwhile, had rounded the clubhouse and was approaching the practice green that lay behind it. Someone large and female was engaged there in polishing her chip shots, and as he paused to watch he stood astounded at her virtuosity. A chip shot, he was aware, having read his Johnny Farrell, is a crisp hit with the clubhead stopping at the ball and not following through. 'Open your stance,' says the venerable Farrell. 'Place your weight on the left foot and hit down at the ball,' and this was precisely what this substantial female was doing. Each ball she struck dropped on the green like a poached egg, and as she advanced to pick them up he saw that she was Agnes Flack.

A loud gasp escaped Cyril. The dream world of breathtaking beauty pirouetted before his eyes as if Arthur Murray were teaching it dancing in a hurry. He was conscious of strange, tumultuous emotions stirring within him. Then the mists cleared, and gazing at Agnes Flack he knew that there before him stood his destined mate. A novelist she might be and no doubt as ghastly a novelist as ever set finger to typewriter key, but what of that? Quite possibly she would grow out of it in time, and in any case he felt that as a man who went about shooting sixty-twos in medal contests he owed it to himself to link his lot with a golfer of her calibre. Theirs would be the ideal union.

In a situation like this no publisher hesitates. A moment later, Cyril was on the green, his arms as far around Agnes Flack as they would go.

'Old girl,' he said. 'You're a grand bit of work!'

Two courses were open to Agnes Flack. She could draw herself to her full height, say 'Sir!' and strike this clinging vine with her number seven iron, or, remembering that Cyril was a publisher and that she had a top copy and two carbons of a novel in her suitcase, she could co-operate and accept his addresses. She chose the latter alternative, and when Cyril suggested that they should spend the honeymoon in Scotland, playing all the famous courses there, she said that that would suit her perfectly. If, as she plighted her troth, a thought of Sidney McMurdo came into her mind, it was merely the renewed conviction that he was an oaf and a fathead temperamentally incapable of recognising good literature when it was handed to him on a skewer.

These passionate scenes take it out of a man, and it is not surprising that Cyril's first move on leaving Agnes Flack should have been in the direction of the bar. Arriving there, he found Professor Farmer steeping himself, as was his custom, in lemon squashes. The warm weather engendered thirst, and since he had come to the Paradise Hotel the straw had seldom left his lips.

'Ah, Cyril, if you don't mind me calling you Cyril, though you will be the first to admit that it's hell of a name,' said the Professor. 'How did everything come out?'

'Quite satisfactorily, Pepperidge. The returns are not all in, but I think I must have won the medal. I shot a sixty-two, which, subtracting my handicap, gives me a thirty-eight. I doubt if anyone will do better than thirty-eight.'

'Most unlikely.'

'Thirty-four under par takes a lot of beating.'

'Quite a good deal. I congratulate you.'

'And that's not all. I'm engaged to the most wonderful girl.'

'Really? I congratulate you again. Who is she?'

'Her name is Agnes Flack.'

The Professor started, dislodging a drop of lemon squash from his lower lip.

'Agnes Flack?'

'Yes.'

'You couldn't be mistaken in the name?'

'No.'

'H'm!'

'Why do you say H'm?'

'I was thinking of Sidney McMurdo.'

'How does he get into the act?'

'He is — or was — betrothed to Agnes Flack, and I am told he has rather a short way with men who get engaged to his fiancée, even if technically ex. Do you know a publisher called Pickering?'

'Harold Pickering? I've met him.'

'He got engaged to Agnes Flack, and it was only by butting Sidney McMurdo in the stomach with his head and disappearing over the horizon that he was able to avoid being torn by the latter into little pieces. But for his ready resource he would have become converted into, as one might say, a sort of publishing hash, though, of course, McMurdo might simply have jumped on him with spiked shoes.'

It was Cyril's turn to say H'm, and he said it with a good deal of thoughtful fervour. He had parted so recently from Sidney McMurdo that he had not had time to erase from his mental retina what might be called the overall picture of him. The massive bulk of Sidney McMurdo rose before his eyes, as did the other's rippling muscles. The discovery that in addition to possessing the physique of a gorilla he had also that animal's easily aroused temper was not one calculated to induce a restful peace of mind. Given the choice between annoying Sidney McMurdo and stirring up a nest of hornets with a fountain pen, he would unhesitatingly have cast his vote for the hornets.

And it was as he sat trying to think what was to be done for the best that the door flew open and the bar became full of McMurdo. He seemed to permeate its every nook and cranny. Nor had Professor Farmer erred in predicting that his mood would be edgy. His eyes blazed, his ears wiggled and a clicking sound like the manipulation of castanets by a Spanish dancer told that he was gnashing his teeth. Except that he was not beating his chest with both fists, he resembled in every respect the gorilla to which Cyril had mentally compared him.

'Ha!' he said, sighting Cyril.

'Oh, hullo, Sidney.'

'Less of the Sidney!' snarled McMurdo. 'I don't want a man of your kidney calling me Sidney,' he went on, rather surprisingly dropping into poetry. 'Agnes Flack tells me she is engaged to you.'

Cyril replied nervously that there had been some informal conversation along those lines.

'She says you hugged her.'

'Only a little.'

'And kissed her.'

'In the most respectful manner.'

'In other words, you have sneaked behind my back like a slithery serpent and stolen from me the woman I love. Perhaps if you have a moment to spare, you will step outside.'

Cyril did not wish to step outside, but it seemed that there was no alternative. He preceded Sidney McMurdo through the door, and was surprised on reaching the wide open spaces to find that Professor Farmer had joined the party. The Professor was regarding Sidney with that penetrating gaze of his which made him look like Boris Karloff on one of his bad mornings.

'Might I ask you to look me in the eye for a moment, Mr. McMurdo,' he said. 'Thank you. Yes, as I thought. You are drowsy. Your eyes are closing. You are falling asleep.'

'No, I'm not.'

'Yes, you are.'

'By Jove, I believe you're right,' said Sidney McMurdo, sinking slowly into a conveniently placed deck chair. 'Yes, I think I'll take a nap.'

The Professor continued to weave arabesques in the air with his hands, and suddenly Sidney McMurdo sat up. His eye rested on Cyril, but it was no longer the flaming eye it had been. Almost affectionate it seemed, and when he spoke his voice was mild.

'Mr. Grooly.'

'On the spot.'

'I have been thinking it over, Mr. Grooly, and I have reached a decision which, though painful, I am sure is right. It is wrong to think only of self. There are times when a man must make the great sacrifice no matter what distress it causes him. You love Agnes Flack, Agnes loves you, and I must not come between you. Take her, Mr. Grooly. I yield her to you, yield her freely. It breaks my heart, but her happiness is all that matters. Take her, Grooly, and if a broken man's blessing is of any use to you, I give it without reserve. I think I'll go to the bar and have a gin and tonic,' said Sidney McMurdo, and proceeded to do so.

'A very happy conclusion to your afternoon's activities,' said Professor Farmer as the swing door closed behind him. 'I often say that there is nothing like hypnotism for straightening out these little difficulties. I thought McMurdo's speech of renunciation was very well phrased, didn't you? In perfect taste. Well, as you will now no longer have need of my services, I suppose I had better de-hypnotise you. It will not be painful, just a momentary twinge,' said the Professor, blowing a lemon-squash-charged breath in Cyril's face, and Cyril was aware of an odd feeling of having been hit by an atom bomb while making a descent in an express elevator. He found himself a little puzzled by his companion's choice of the expression 'momentary twinge', but he had not leisure to go into what was after all a side issue. With the removal of the hypnotic spell there had come to him the realisation of the unfortunate position in which he had placed himself, and he uttered a sharp 'Oh, golly!'

'I beg your pardon?' said the Professor.

'Listen,' said Cyril, and his voice shook like a jelly in a high wind. 'Does it count if you ask a girl to marry you when you're hypnotised?'

'You are speaking of Miss Flack?'

'Yes, I proposed to her on the practice green, carried away by the super-excellence of her chip shots, and I can't stand the sight of her. And, what's more, in about three weeks I'm supposed to be marrying someone else. You remember Patricia Binstead, the girl who showed you into my office?'

'Very vividly.'

'She holds the copyright. What am I to do? You couldn't go and hypnotise Agnes Flack and instil her, as you call it, with the idea that I'm the world's leading louse, could you?'

'My dear fellow, nothing easier.'

'Then do it without an instant's delay,' said Cyril. 'Tell her I'm scratch and pretended to have a twenty-four handicap in order to win the medal. Tell her I'm sober only at the rarest intervals. Tell her I'm a Communist spy and my name's really Golinsky. Tell her I've two wives already, but you'll know what to say.'

He waited breathlessly for the Professor's return.

'Well?' he cried.

'All washed up, my dear Cyril. I left her reunited to McMurdo. She says she wouldn't marry you if you were the last publisher on earth and wouldn't let you sponsor her novel if you begged her on bended knees. She says she is going to let Simon and Schuster have it, and she hopes that will be a lesson to you.'

Cyril drew a deep breath.

'Pepperidge, you're wonderful!'

'One does one's best,' said the Professor modestly. 'Well now that the happy ending has been achieved, how about returning to the bar? I'll buy you a lemon squash.'

'Do you really like that stuff?'

'I love it.'

It was on the tip of Cyril's tongue to say that one would have thought he was a man who would be more likely to share Count Dracula's preference for human blood when thirsty, but he refrained from putting the thought into words. It might, he felt, be lacking in tact, and after all, why criticise a man for looking like something out of a horror film if his heart was so patently of the purest gold. It is the heart that matters, not the features, however unshuffled.

'I'm with you,' he said. 'A lemon squash would be most refreshing.'

'They serve a very good lemon squash here.'

'Probably made from contented lemons.'

'I shouldn't wonder,' said the Professor.

He smiled a hideous smile. It had just occurred to him that if he hypnotised the waiter, he would be spared the necessity of disbursing money, always a consideration to a man of slender means.

P. G. WODEHOUSE

JOY IN THE MORNING

Bertie Wooster was trapped in Steeple Bumpleigh.

With him were Florence Craye to whom he had once been engaged; 'Stilton' Cheesewright to whom Florence was now promised and who regarded Bertie as a snake in the grass; Zenobia Hopwood and her guardian Lord Worpledon; and, biggest blot of all on the landscape, Edwin the Boy Scout, doing acts of kindness out of sheer malevolence.

Complete disaster could only be averted by the genius of Jeeves who, at the moment of crisis, extricated the young master with a stratagem as smoothly executed as it was brilliantly conceived.

P. G. WODEHOUSE

JEEVES AND THE FEUDAL SPIRIT

Jeeves did not approve of Bertie Wooster's new moustache, and expressed himself in such terms on the matter that some feeling of coolness between him and his employer could not fail to result.

Then the thunder-clouds began to gather from another direction, and Wooster thought that he might have to face the impending crisis alone. But Jeeves was not the man to allow a domestic tiff to come between him and their common enemy. The feudal spirit burned bright within him and he rallied to his master's cause as resourcefully and impeturbably as ever before.

CORONET BOOKS

ALSO AVAILABLE FROM CORONET BOOKS

P. G. WODEHOUSE

☐	23830 5	Sunset At Blandings	£1.25
☐	21789 8	Jeeves And The Feudal Spirit	£1.25
☐	21790 1	Thank You, Jeeves	£1.25
☐	21788 X	Joy In The Morning	£1.25
☐	32821 5	Barmy In Wonderland	£1.50
☐	32820 7	Ice In The Bedroom	£1.50
☐	33210 7	Ring For Jeeves	£1.50
☐	22696 X	Mr Mulliner Speaking	£1.50

JAMES HILTON

☐	04359 8	Goodbye Mr Chips	95p

Ed. GEOFFREY JAGGARD

☐	23680 9	Wooster's World	£1.25

All these books are available at your local bookshop or newsagent, or can be ordered direct from the publisher. Just tick the titles you want and fill in the form below.

Prices and availability subject to change without notice.

CORONET BOOKS, P.O. Box 11, Falmouth, Cornwall.

Please send cheque or postal order, and allow the following for postage and packing:

U.K. – 45p for one book, plus 20p for the second book, and 14p for each additional book ordered up to a £1.63 maximum.

B.F.P.O. and EIRE – 45p for the first book, plus 20p for the second book, and 14p per copy for the next 7 books, 8p per book thereafter.

OTHER OVERSEAS CUSTOMERS – 75p for the first book, plus 21p per copy for each additional book.

Name ....

Address ....

....